Mary (Savory) Lady Elvey

Life and Reminiscences of George J. Elvey

Mary (Savory) Lady Elvey

Life and Reminiscences of George J. Elvey

ISBN/EAN: 9783337095079

Printed in Europe, USA, Canada, Australia, Japan

Cover: Foto ©Raphael Reischuk / pixelio.de

More available books at **www.hansebooks.com**

LIFE

AND

REMINISCENCES

OF

GEORGE J. ELVEY

KNT.

MUS. DOC. OXON. ETC.

LATE ORGANIST TO H.M. QUEEN VICTORIA, AND FORTY-SEVEN
YEARS ORGANIST OF ST. GEORGE'S CHAPEL, WINDSOR

BY

LADY ELVEY

ILLUSTRATED

LONDON

SAMPSON LOW, MARSTON & COMPANY, LIMITED

St. Dunstan's House

FETTER LANE, FLEET STREET, E.C.

1894

PREFACE.

THE compiling of the following Memoir has been no easy task, for my dear husband, ever averse to publicity, practically destroyed the whole of his large correspondence, and kept no diary. It was frequently represented to him how interesting the publication of his reminiscences would prove, and although he often said he could fill a volume with the strange things he had seen and heard in his eventful life and long cathedral experiences, he strenuously objected to do so, fearing to cause pain to others or to reveal the unlimited confidence always placed in him. When he went to Windsor his brother's parting words were, " Do not open your mouth to fill other people's." To this sage advice he always strictly adhered.

Should, therefore, the volume not meet the expectations of the reader, I must crave their forbearance on the ground above mentioned. I have been almost entirely dependent upon my memory for facts, and upon such help as many of my husband's friends and pupils could render me.   Their kindness I would here thankfully record, especially that of my husband's favourite niece, Miss Evelyn M. Savory, and of Mr. C. G. Verrinder, Mus. Doc.

At first it seemed almost beyond my power to give any true idea of Sir George's life; yet if this simple record be the slightest incentive in inducing others to follow his example in consecrating to the Master whom he so dearly loved, all their life and talents, I shall feel amply repaid.

MARY ELVEY.

TABLE OF CONTENTS.

CHAPTER VI.

CHAPTER VII.

CHAPTER VIII.

CHAPTER IX.

CHAPTER X.

Chapter XI.

Chapter XII.

Chapter XIII.

Chapter XIV.

Chapter XV.

Chapter XVI.

CHAPTER XXII.

CHAPTER XXIII.

CHAPTER XXIV.

CHAPTER XXV.

CHAPTER XXVI.

CHAPTER XXVII.

Chapter XXVIII.

Chapter XXIX.

Chapter XXX.

Chapter XXXI.

Chapter XXXII.

Chapter XXXIII.

Chapter XXXIV.

Chapter XXXV.

Chapter XXXVI.

Chapter XXXVII.

Chapter XXXVIII.

Chapter XXXIX.

LIST OF ILLUSTRATIONS.

GEORGE J. ELVEY, Knt., Mus. Doc.

CHAPTER I.

IN a small house in Union Street, Canterbury, on the north side of the cathedral, George Job Elvey was born on Wednesday, March 27th, 1816. For generations his ancestors had lived in and around the ancient city. His grandfather, Stephen Elvey, was a very fine-looking old man, distinguishable by a Roman nose and fair complexion. He was remarkable for good temper, and his children used to say they had never heard him make a complaint.

Early in life he left the Church of England on conscientious grounds, and attended chapel. At this, his uncle, Mr. Lawrence, with whom he had lived, and who intended him for his heir, was so angry that he altered his will, and cut him off with a shilling.

Stephen Elvey had two sons,—one was for twenty-five years minister of Elim Chapel, Fetter Lane, London, and, it is interesting to note, was uncle to Thos. Sidney Cooper, R.A., as well as to the subject of this memoir. The other, John Elvey, married in 1799 Abigail Hardiman, by whom he had nine children, five boys and four girls, of whom George was the seventh.

Only four children lived to maturity, but all from infancy showed considerable musical talent. Indeed, the name of Elvey seems for centuries to have been connected with music in Canterbury. Amongst the records of the monks of the late " Monastery of Chryst Church, Canterbury, with their offices, rewards, and pensions " occurs the following entry :

" Chaunter : Johannes Elphe (Peti-Canon)."

We further read, that at the dissolution he received the magnificent pension of £3 6s. 3d. !

John and Abigail Elvey being Dissenters, George was baptized in the Presbyterian Chapel on April 14th.

His mother seems to have been a very godly woman, and Sir George used often to repeat the words she said to him on her deathbed : " Satan has been very busy, but I am on the Rock."

Doubtless he and his brother owed much to her Christian training and character, which appears to have impressed them very deeply—although George was only a boy of fourteen when he left his home to go to Oxford.

Concerning his father, we learn that he was a very talented man, and his son often used to say that he had never heard anyone who could so well play country-dances on the violin.

The following account of Sir George's early life is best given in his own words, as written down by Lady Elvey when he was seventy-four years of age :

"I have heard my brother say that the first sign I showed of having an ear for music, was imitating my father sing : ' Arm, arm, ye brave!' and which, as a child, not catching the words, I sang, ' Toll, Toll, ye brave.'

" My poor brother, when I was only six, met with a sad misadventure, being accidentally shot by a friend (whose sister he afterwards married). He was taken to the Kent and Canterbury Hospital, where his leg was amputated.

" During the time he remained there, I used to be taken up to see him. He always made me sing to him, but, being very nervous, I never could do so without hiding my head in the curtains of his bed.

"At that time I invented a little tune, which used to be called ' Toody, Tady.'

(A facsimile of this, as written by Sir George from memory in his seventy-fourth year, is given below.)

"At an early age I was admitted as a chorister into Canterbury Cathedral under Highmore Skeats. Here I soon distinguished myself by taking a prominent part in the services. The first solo I sung in the cathedral was, ' Oh! come, let us worship!' abridged from one of the Chandos Anthems. I have been told that I was a very pretty boy, and from the time I sung this solo I was in great request for concerts and musical entertainments.

"During my early days in the choir the service was held in the Sermon-house, or Chapter House."

(The name Sermon-house seems to have been given to it in the reign of Henry VIII., when, instead of a numerous fraternity, the Chapter was reduced to a dean and twelve prebends.

Such a large room not being required for Chapter business, it was fitted up for a sermon-house, with a pulpit, pews, and galleries.

So early was this, that the chief gallery, with latticed casements (the Royal Closet), is dated 1554, the 36th of Henry VIII. For many years the congregation, after prayers in the choir, used to retire here for the sermon, but this was found so inconvenient that the practice was discontinued until the time of King James II.

The Lord Chancellor Jeffreys then informed the Chapter that the Presbyterians had a petition before the King and Council, representing it as a place of little or no use, and desiring that they might have it for their meeting-house.

The person entrusted with this message being a member of the choir proposed their making it the chapel for early prayers, which were read every day in the week, and, till then, in the choir. " This will do," said the Chancellor ; " advise your dean and prebendaries from me to have it put to that use immediately, for if the Presbyterians don't get it, perhaps others will, whom you may like worse.")

" Talking of this, in going down to the Sermon-house to turn the books for the service one morning, I caught a young jackdaw. My intention was to have returned and deposited Jack until after service in the cupboard where the surplices were kept. Instead of this, however, I met the procession, and I had no alternative but to join in, with the bird stowed away under my surplice. (By the way, in those days we used to wear full surplices, and frills round our necks.) I deposited him on a ledge where we kept our books, and for a time he was quite quiet, but unfortunately he was intoxicated by the music, and, toppling off the ledge, boldly walked between the two sides of the choir, and after indulging in various noises, took his flight up to the roof with a loud ' caw,' much to the astonishment of the congregation, but to my intense horror. Service ended, I moved out with the procession in no enviable frame of mind. However, fortunately for me, my brother was master of the boys at this time, and he, knowing that the account I gave of the adventure was correct, could with difficulty conceal his own merriment, and soon succeeded in making my peace with the authorities.

" Subsequently I recovered the bird, and took

him home, where I taught him various tricks. He became very knowing, but after some time he annoyed my brother, who incontinently wrung his neck, to the great grief of my mother and myself.

"I do not think I have anything remarkable to tell of my early career, but I remember one or two things which may be amusing.

"As a boy I was devoted to soldiers—a predisposition which, on one occasion, led me into an awkward scrape. I had been away from the cathedral for several days on sick leave, but was returning to school one morning, when I met some boys who told me that a review was to take place on the Downs that day. I at once told my friends they must excuse me to my master on the plea of illness, and they quietly went to school, while I started off to enjoy the sport. But, as ill-luck would have it, the master, grieved to hear such a poor account of his favourite pupil, went after lessons to my home, and anxiously inquired for me. My mother was greatly surprised, and assured him that I was better, and had gone to school.

"As I was returning the boys met me, in great consternation, and we at once held a solemn council, fearing that we should be severely punished, as our master was somewhat violent at times.

"As head-boy I duly instructed my companions what to do when they should be summoned into the master's presence. As we stood before him, fearful of the consequences, Mr. Skeats in a solemn voice said: 'Well, boys, what do you think you deserve now?'

Anticipating punishment, with one voice we exclaimed: 'A good thrashing, sir!' This frank and unexpected admission so disarmed his wrath that with a 'Good boys, good boys, you may go home,' we were dismissed, not a little to our satisfaction and delight."

(Throughout his life Sir George took great interest in military display, which was somewhat curious, considering how peace-loving he was.)

"One other curious circumstance I remember of my early years.

"A certain Mr. Greene was to make a balloon ascent one afternoon from the Dane-John Hill in Canterbury.

"Crowds of people were expected to witness the sight, the inhabitants having subscribed to inflate the balloon with gas.

"As I was crossing the Dane-John in the

morning, I saw the balloon there, and quite accidentally discovered in its side a tiny hole, whence
the gas was escaping.   I told this to the balloonist,
who straightway got into the car, and at once
commenced his ascent, much to the surprise and
disappointment of the people, as the balloon was
advertised to ascend at three o'clock, and they had
calculated on promenading the Dane-John until
that hour."

CHAPTER II.

WHEN I was a chorister in Canterbury Cathedral, there was an old woman about the place who was nicknamed 'Mam Godlybooks,' for, if anyone appeared in the cathedral without a book, she quickly supplied the deficiency. On one occasion a man peeped in during service time, when the old lady shouted out, 'Come in, there's plenty of room.' And so there was, for she was almost the only individual in the cathedral.

"Another curious old lady I remember in Canterbury was one who, although possessed of considerable property, was a great miser.

" She used to search in the streets for anything which it was possible to turn to account, and was particularly fond of collecting the ends of tallow candles.

" The people of Canterbury, who were well aware of her wealth, used to flatter her and invite her out to tea, hoping by this means to procure for themselves favourable mention in her will.

"These invitations were accepted, and in winter-time she used to carry a lantern, minus a candle. When the time for departure arrived, she would exclaim, 'Oh! dear, I quite forgot to put any candle in my lantern, would you mind giving me a piece?' This was done, and the lantern lighted, but directly Betty got out of sight, she blew it out, and stowed the candle in her pocket.

"Rumour said she had once been married, and had starved her husband. Certain it is she starved her horses (for she kept a carriage, such as it was) until the animals had to be put an end to.

"Betty would sometimes walk all the way from Canterbury to Rochester, to the Traveller's Shelter, in order to procure the fourpence which was given to the inmates in the morning, after a free night's lodging.

"One of the Canons, thinking to gain some advantage, paid considerable court to Betty, and offered her a pinch of snuff. For this the old lady was ever grateful, and, when she died, left him her fortune.

"On this becoming known, an old woman, who, it seems, had expectations of the property, wrote a book for the purpose of rendering the Canon un-popular.

"Hoping to appease his detractor, he sent for her, and, when she arrived, looking very beaming and fully expecting to receive a handsome douceur, he quietly said : 'Well, Mrs. Blank, I have been thinking of doing something for you. I wish to give you this chair, so that you can sit down easy for life.'

"Whilst I was a chorister, there was much difference of opinion among the Canons about the position of the organ in the cathedral. Those who wished for its removal took advantage of the absence of their most strenuous opponent to have the alteration effected, giving no little annoyance to this gentleman when he again came into resi-dence. This trick continuing to be a very sore subject with him, he was delighted when any inconvenience was experienced from the instru-ment. Sometimes it would take to ciphering, and this was an especial pleasure to him, for, although deaf, he never failed to hear this noise, and would then remark, in loud tones, to his brother Canon, sitting on the other side of the choir : 'Is that that *argan* again?' "

CHAPTER III.

THE choir of the cathedral at this period was in a very efficient state, and many of our noble services were performed without accompaniment.

George Elvey was solo boy nearly the whole of the time he was in the choir, and he had the power possessed by few boys, of embellishing the music, where required, with as flexible a shake as possessed by any professional lady singer. His voice was powerful, and of beautiful quality; added to this, he sung with an amount of feeling and expression rarely heard.

The following interesting reminiscences were given in the course of an interview with an old man upwards of eighty years of age, now in Chelsea Hospital, and once a fellow-chorister with Sir George Elvey at Canterbury:

"I knew Sir George Elvey well; I remember him as a boy at Canterbury. We used to sing in the choir together. George was a *nice* lad, not fond of noise and bluster as some boys are, but very quiet and gentle in his manner.

" He was always fond of music, and glad to get home to his practice. He had a beautiful voice, sang all the solos, and took the chief part in the services. Ah! and he could *shake*, you know— when the music said ' shake,' he could do it—we could not. It's many years ago now, and things have faded into a kind of dream, but I can distinctly remember his beautiful singing, nor shall I ever forget it."

To return to Sir George's own words :

" When I was fourteen, my brother (who had been master of the choristers in Canterbury Cathedral) was appointed organist of New College, Oxford, and, as he did not know what was to become of me, thought it better that I should leave the choir (although my voice was not broken), in order that it should not be strained.

" It was not a rule at Canterbury in those days to give any gratuity to a boy when he left the choir, but in consequence of my meritorious (! !) services the Dean and Chapter awarded me the munificent sum of £15 towards carrying on my musical education.

" The first instrument I learnt to play, long before

I left the choir was the violin, and as a little fellow some of our acquaintances used to be called in to hear me play 'Bluebeard's March,' which I was thought to perform in good style."

In the autumn of 1830, young Elvey and his brother quitted the scenes of their childhood at Canterbury, to which town they never again returned, except on temporary visits.

Sir George would describe in later years his surprise and astonishment on his first arrival at London Bridge by coach, *en route* for Oxford, at the scene of bustle and "hurrying to and fro," which was even at that time to be seen in the marvellous city.

He could think of nothing which more adequately represented the scene than Handel's chorus :

> "All we like sheep have gone astray,
> We have turned every one to his own way."

This idea so impressed him that he recalled it when walking with a companion in the streets of London more than fifty years afterwards.

When Dr. Stephen Elvey took up his duties at Oxford, the New College choir was very destitute of good singers, and he was glad to avail himself of the services of his young brother George, and often called upon him to sing the solos in the chapel.

A lady, speaking of young Elvey at this time, wrote thus to him many years after:

"I remember you as a tall, shy lad with a beautiful voice joining in some glees at my brother's rooms in New College one evening, Dr. Elvey playing. One of the pieces sung was, 'Then round about the starry throne,' and another, 'Now the bright Morning Star.' I recollect it as if it were only yesterday. The pieces sunk deeply into my memory."

*　　*　　*　　*　　*

While at Oxford, George Elvey commenced the study of the piano, and speaking of this he says:

"At this time the piano was very trying to me, for I had been able to read music fluently since I was eleven, and knew exactly how it *ought* to be played, but my fingers refused to draw forth the sounds I knew they should.

"Several times I fled from the instrument, driven wild by my performances, but my brother sent me back, with a box on the ear, to plod on at what he knew was so essential to my future success.

"I was at this time very fond of composing,

but my brother discouraged my spending much time over this until I became thoroughly proficient on the piano and organ.

"He would, however, take me with him to the Bodleian Library, where we had permission to examine the old music (which was brought to us in clothes-baskets), and here he would call upon me to sing over a good deal of it to him. This I could do without the least trouble, and the time thus spent was very enjoyable, while the knowledge gained proved afterwards very useful to me.

"I have mentioned that I had learnt the violin when I was very young, and this was a great thing for me at Oxford, for I was frequently able to take part in good concerts, playing either viola or violin."

It was at Oxford that Sir George learnt the various times of Handel's music, both from his brother and from Dr. Crotch, with whom he was intimate.

Concerning this, Sir George wrote the following account in 1872 to a friend:

"Dr. Crotch told my late brother that he marked the time of Handel's choruses from Randall of Cambridge, who played (I believe the viola) in Handel's orchestra."

Thus Sir George received the time in a direct line from the grand old Saxon.

Whilst living with his brother at Oxford (who, besides being a splendid musician, was a humble-minded Christian), George Elvey was deeply impressed with a sermon he heard from the Rev. Rowland Hill in Oxford, only two or three weeks before the latter's death.

George was at this time only seventeen, but the impression made upon him by the wonderful discourse from such an aged saint of God remained with him to the close of his life. The following account of the sermon was written by Sir George Elvey at the age of seventy-six, and is an instance of the remarkable memory he possessed :

"Some time in March, Rowland Hill preached in Oxford, in Market Street Chapel, near the church of St. Peter-le-Bailey. This was within a very short time of his death, which occurred April 11th, 1833. My dear brother, his wife, and one or two others went to hear him. We had gone out to tea with some ladies close by, and when there, hearing that Rowland Hill was to preach, the whole party, including myself, attended the service. He was at that time very feeble, and it was with some little difficulty he was got into the pulpit.

When there, he had to sit; his venerable and saintlike appearance I can never forget.

"He opened his sermon by telling the people they had come to hear the dying speech of an old man. For his text he took Hebrews I. 2, 3, and it was undoubtedly a fine sermon on the Divinity of Christ. I remember, when quoting the passage, 'He shall reign until He hath put all enemies under His feet,' he struck his breast exclaiming, 'His enemies in *me*.' At the end of the sermon the preacher said, 'Hear how the Church people pray,' and repeated the Collect, 'Blessed Lord, who hast caused all holy Scriptures,' etc., and enlarged upon it, particularly the passage, 'Read, mark, learn, and inwardly digest.' The chapel was very full; several undergraduates were present, and myself with many others had to stand all the time.

"Truly he was a man of God.

"G. J. ELVEY.

"*June 8th*, 1892."

*   *   *   *   *

One Sunday, when dining with the Queen's Band after chapel service, Dr. Elvey related a story of a confirmed atheist, who, calling upon

Rowland Hill to discuss theological questions, was asked by the divine whether he believed in the Ten Commandments. The person addressed, determined to maintain a consistent position, said, "No." At this Rowland Hill called a servant and said, "Show this gentleman the door, and be careful that he does not take anything."

As Dr. Elvey finished the tale, one of the gentlemen present jumped up and said, "That is perfectly true, sir; the atheist was my uncle."

CHAPTER IV.

BEFORE he was nineteen, George had made such progress in his musical studies that he was constantly in request to take temporary duty at Christ Church Cathedral, Magdalen, and New College Chapels in Oxford. His brother, considering him a thoroughly good organist, was looking out for a suitable opening for him when the vacancy occurred at St. George's Chapel, Windsor, through the death of Mr. Skeats. Backed by a dozen or more splendid testimonials, he was readily accepted to compete for this important post.

Mr. Spencer Braham thus wrote to Mr. Gore :

" Elvey is, indeed, a most talented young man, and his character unexceptionable. Our Dean has promised to write by to-night's post to Mr. Cust, one of your Canons, in commendation of him. He, though young, has all the steadiness and soberness of an older person."

*　　　*　　　*　　　*　　　*

" I have much pleasure in testifying that George Elvey has the greatest knowledge of music, is a very excellent performer on the organ, and in every way able to conduct a choir. I may also add that he is a person of the most irreproachable character, and it would be a personal satisfaction to me if he should succeed in the attainment of any object in life by which his future prospects would be advanced.

"C. MEREDITH,
"Fellow of Lincoln College."

Accordingly, on April 26th, 1835, George Elvey in fear and trembling left Oxford for Windsor by coach. That night, spent at the Adelaide Hotel in Sheet Street, he never forgot, so intense was the anxiety he went through as to the result of the coming trial. Next morning, arrayed in a blue tail-coat with brass buttons and a yellow waistcoat, he presented himself at the Chapel Royal, such a timid, bashful boy, that all treated his daring to compete with the distinguished men who had entered the arena, as a joke, never for a moment imagining that he would outstrip his numerous co-competitors. Among these were Sir George Smart, Sir Henry Bishop, Philip Knight, composer of " She wore a wreath of roses," Dr.

Hodges, and Dr. Sebastian Wesley. The latter, already sore at having been defeated by him in the Gresham competition, never forgave Sir George for the second defeat he experienced at his hands. By the way, the anthem he sent in for the Gresham Prize, when Dr. Elvey gained it, was "The Wilderness," which, scored all over as it was by the examiners, he had framed and hung in his room.

When Elvey's time for organ trial came, he was dismayed to find the pedals of the organ covered with a board, while the stool slanted so much that any attempt to use the former resulted in the player's nose coming in unpleasant contact with the manuals. After the first experiment Elvey turned the stool, and balancing himself on the sharp edge, made such use of the pedals that the lay-clerks called him "a thunder-and-lightning player," expressing the opinion—doubtless based on his youth—that he would never do.

Among the pieces he performed on this occasion was a fugue by Bach.

One of the gentlemen on trial had already been defeated by Dr. Stephen Elvey at Oxford, and the latter used often to laugh and say, "I not only conquered him myself, but I made a man to conquer him." Only one stood the smallest chance against young Elvey, and this was not from ability, but because one of the canons was determined to have, if possible, a candidate of his own appointed.

This rev. gentleman was so vexed at being defeated, that for many years he lost no opportunity of annoying Mr. Elvey, who indeed felt the slights so keenly, that even to within a few weeks of his death it pained him much to speak of what he then went through. Elvey at the same time, however, spoke with pleasure of the kindness of another member of the Chapter, who ably defended him, to the ultimate routing of his enemy.

The officials seem to have had scant regard for the comfort of the candidates, and at the end of the contest no luncheon was offered them, which called forth a remark from Mr. Gore, that it was left to the despised Minor Canons to provide refreshment. He therefore courteously offered the hospitality of his house to Elvey, Philip Knight, and some others.

In the evening after the trial, the Dean and some of the Chapter were dining with the King (who claimed the final vote respecting the appointment), and he inquired about the candidates. On being told that Elvey was the best, but was too young, he replied, " The best man is to have it ; " and when, on future occasions, young Elvey was spoken of in glowing terms, he used to say, " Ah ! I appointed him ! " At this time Elvey was just nineteen years of age.

The delight of George's elder brother, Stephen, when the tidings reached Oxford of the former's appointment, can be better imagined than described.   He was waiting at the stage-office when the coach arrived, and, on hearing the news from the conductor, he waved his hat in the air, and fairly shouted for joy.

From the time of Elvey's appointment William IV. and Queen Adelaide took a great interest in the young organist, who entertained in his turn a warm affection and respect for them, as they ever treated him with the greatest kindness and consideration.   He was frequently in request at the Castle, and often spent the evening playing to the King, when the latter was suffering from rheumatic gout.   When otherwise unoccupied his chief delight would be to gather two or three friends around him for a musical evening.   Mr. William Corden (artist to Her Majesty and the Prince Consort), who was Sir George's first pupil on the violin, still speaks of the enjoyment they had in playing Corelli's Trios and other music at his house in the Cloisters.

Sir George moved here shortly after he arrived in Windsor, having previously occupied rooms in the Curfew Tower, a somewhat gloomy abode for a solitary young man.

His new home being so high above the surrounding country, was much exposed to the weather, and the howling of the wind through the doors and windows at night sometimes nearly drove him wild. Once, when, in spite of his entreaties, the winds refused to resolve a chord which they had been murmuring or howling half the night, he sprang out of bed, and hurrying down to the piano, resolved it for them, exclaiming, " There, that's it !"

One subject of interest in connection with the Castle at Windsor is perhaps not very generally known.

Under the old laws, Windsor being a royal residence, anyone living within the precincts was exempt from arrest on account of debt.

In consequence of this, certain gentlemen took up their abode there to avoid their creditors ; and Sir George used to tell how some men in his early days were located in rooms in the Belfry Tower, one titled individual living with the father of Mr. Montagu Williams, who was then a resident in the Cloisters. (Mr. Montagu Williams, in his " Reminiscences," speaks of " Dr. Elvey " as one of his father's friends.) Sir George would recount how these refugees amused themselves by taunting the sheriff's officers, venturing as near as possible to the outskirts of the Castle grounds, and then inviting these men to arrest them.

On one occasion the sheriffs got the better of them, and by means of a little plot succeeded in making some arrests. According to law, Sunday was their one day of freedom, when they could leave their sanctuary with safety until midnight.

In this particular instance, a number had chartered a vehicle, and, like all sons of freedom, wished to be absent from their prison as long as possible. They therefore just timed their return for about midnight. The officers got news of this, and hiring a substantial waggon, met the party as they were returning over Dorney Common in the darkness, and with much good-nature precipitated a collision.

As midnight was close upon them, the poor debtors took to their heels and made for the Castle.

The fatal strokes of twelve, however, pealed out before they could get inside, much to the delight of the sheriff's officers, who promptly arrested them.

This anecdote, and many others with which Sir George used to amuse his listeners, show what a connecting link he was between the present and a past in which the conditions of life were so vastly different.

CHAPTER V.

A FEW months after his appointment to
Windsor it was announced that the young
organist had been successful in gaining the gold
medal offered for competition by the Professor of
Music at Gresham College.

This success had really been won in the competition of 1834, but the presentation of the medal
was not made till July 14th of this year. The
ceremony took place in the Town Hall, and attracted a considerable concourse of people. The
prize composition was an anthem for five voices
from the 86th Psalm, "Bow down thine ear, O
Lord!" and it had previously been performed at
the afternoon service in St. George's Chapel.

The presentation of the medal was accompanied
by an address from Mr. Horsley, couched in the
following words :

"Mr. George Elvey, in the absence of the
Gresham Professor of Music, whose advanced age
prevents him from attending here to-day, it is my

grateful office to present you with this medal. It is highly gratifying to you, sir, and to me, as an English musician, to know that there are persons who have a taste for the highest and noblest productions of our art, and who are ready to hold out every inducement for their cultivation and encouragement. You have well responded to their good intentions. Your anthem, which we have just heard, is calculated to do you the greatest credit, whether we consider it in regard to conception or execution. The style is truly ecclesiastical, the construction of the parts shows that you have carefully studied good authors, and that your mind is imbued with their excellences.

" There is one circumstance connected with this anthem which I am induced to mention. On former occasions there was always a little discussion between my brother-umpires and myself with regard to the relative merits of the compositions submitted to us, but in your case there was none. We were at once agreed that to you the prize should be given, and I flatter myself that your success with us was not without effect in placing you in the honourable station which you now occupy. You are young, and I trust that you will go on improving. The great name which adorns this medal will stimulate your exertions. May your career be prosperous, may you live in honour, and die in happiness!"

About this time Mr. Elvey received the appointment of organist to Queen Adelaide, and among his earliest pupils were Prince George (the present Duke) of Cambridge and Prince Edward of Saxe-Weimar. For the confirmation of the former he composed by request his anthem, now so popular, "Wherewithal shall a young man cleanse his way," but was uncertain whether his music would be accepted for use on this occasion.

The King, however, having heard it spoken of, very kindly arranged to go down to the Chapel, and sent, greatly to Mr. Elvey's alarm and surprise, the following message, "The King is in the Chapel, and you are to go at once."

At this he rushed off, and upon learning the object of His Majesty's visit, ascended, in fear and trembling, to the organ-loft. He commenced to play, feeling sure that his music *must* be a failure when heard without the voices, and still lower sank his spirits when word was brought that the anthem was to be repeated. When once again the King demanded it, Elvey's spirits sank to zero.

But this feeling was dispelled on descending the

organ-loft stairs, around the entrance to which friends were waiting, eager to pour upon him their congratulations at his wonderful success in having so thoroughly pleased His Majesty.

It is almost needless to add that the anthem was duly performed at the Duke's confirmation.   Of this latter event a very vivid recollection is retained by all now living, who, as choristers, took part in the service; for the kind old King presented them each with a guinea, "to remember," as he said, " that they had been there," and, hearing that one boy, through illness, was unable to be present, the King sent his guinea by a companion, saying that his was "for a remembrance that he had *not* been there."

As a memento of the event Prince George presented Mr. Elvey with a portrait of himself, taken at the time, in his uniform as a Life-guardsman.

A year or two before Elvey's death he met his old pupil, the now Duke of Cambridge, at a City dinner, and was truly pleased and gratified with the kind reception he gave him, showing that he had not forgotten his old master.

The first Christmas Day he was at Windsor, Mr. Elvey was not a little surprised and vexed, on coming down from the organ-loft after service, to see the choir-boys posted at the Chapel doors, trencher in hand, soliciting money from the congregation as they passed out.

Boiling over with indignation at what he considered a most undignified proceeding, he sought the Dean, and protested strongly against their conduct, begging him at once to suppress a practice so derogatory to a Royal Chapel.

This the Dean agreed to do, and from that day the boys had to be satisfied with voluntary and private additions to their pocket-money.

Another thing that worried Elvey a good deal was the slovenly way in which the clergy and choir entered the sacred building. He was a man who could not bear anything which savoured, even unintentionally, of irreverence. But it was not until several years afterwards—indeed, according to a record kept by Mr. French, not until 1846—that the procession was arranged in the present order, and even till 1844 the lay-clerks were in the habit of giving out the anthems instead of the Minor Canons, which appears a somewhat curious arrangement, as they, according to ancient usage, were expected to take an equal share with the lay-clerks in the musical part of the service.

One old custom was continued for a considerable time at St. George's. As soon as the third collect was ended, and the symphony before the anthem commenced, the two or four senior boys took a pile of anthem-books, which were ready turned beside them, and gave them round to the congregation assembled in the stalls. When the Queen was in chapel, as she usually was on Sunday morning, the head boy went up to the royal closet and handed a book to Her Majesty. This, and turning her books before the service, constituted a much-esteemed privilege.

When these anthem-books, which had been used in all the Royal Chapels, were discarded, Queen Victoria ordered a handsomely bound copy to be given to each member of the several choirs.

In the spring of 1836 the Glee Club in London offered a ten-guinea prize for the best serious glee, but omitted to state that only members of the club were allowed to compete. Mr. Elvey sent in a composition, "O Power Supreme," which was examined with the others on the appointed day, and pronounced the winner.

When the name of the author was unfolded, however, he, not being a member of the club, was ineligible to receive the money, and the only reward he had, was being permitted to print on the

title-page of his work that it was the prize composition.

A few days afterwards the following amusing
lines appeared :

"The funds of the Glee Club being in a condition
To afford a reward for a good composition,
The sons of Apollo in conclave agree
That ten pounds shall be giv'n for the best serious glee.
They resolve that the second-best man shall have five.
The design is proclaim'd, and the glees are composed,
Under hieroglyphical emblems enclosed,
Sent in, and perform'd.   The best glee is declared.
The party to hail the composer prepared ;
And all hush'd in suspense, when, the seals being broken,
The disclosure appears a mistake to betoken !
The winner, the moment his name is detected,
Not being a member, of course is rejected.
So that out of the list, which at first numbered three,
The two standing candidates victors must be.
And this comfort they glean from the bottle thus burst,
(On the last day of April instead of the first,)
That as no rival glees will remain for the purse,
None, 'tis plain, can be better than theirs, and none worse.
The joy of the donors has likewise this zest,
That at once they reward both the worst and the best.
'Tis so in a donkey-race, where success depends more
Upon temper than speed.
To fulfil the old adage, though last, yet not least,
The prize is adjudged to the hindermost beast ! "

    *   *   *   *   *

A few weeks later Elvey prepared a cantata for
the King's birthday.

The opening symphony is of a jubilant character leading up to the recitative, " Hark ! what tumultuous sounds," in which the trumpet takes a prominent part.

Then follows a tenor solo, "Oh! the soul-stirring sounds!" In this movement the imitation of the bells by the instruments is the chief feature.

Following this without a break comes the chorus, " The King, the good King!" This is a cheerful and bright example of part-writing.

The fifth number, a fugue, " May the King and his Queen," is written to a bold and vigorous subject, drawing to a climax on the words, " Britain's loud cheer, Huzza ! Huzza !" This was performed at the Castle on August 21st, with full band and chorus, by order of the King.

At this time the present private chapel of the Castle was the music-room, and Elvey frequently took his choir there to give performances.

One night, when they had gone up to sing some glees and madrigals, William IV. came in after dinner, and bowing to the company generally, lay down on the sofa. Then pulling a large silk bandana handkerchief out of his pocket he placed it over his head, and soon fell fast asleep, to the no little surprise and chagrin of the performers.

CHAPTER VI.

AGAIN taking up Sir George's own words : "On my arrival in Windsor on May 1st, 1835, I found things in a very disordered state. There was no bill drawn up for the Chapel, but the service and anthem for each day were fixed by the organist. The senior boy came up into the organ-loft just before the beginning of the service to inquire what was to be rendered. One of the old sextons told me that Dr. Aylward, on one occasion, having appointed the anthem, the choir sent word up that they were unable to sing it, because Mr. —— had a cold. The Doctor returned answer that 'they could do as they liked about singing it, but he intended to play it.'

" The choir was in such a feeble state in my early days that I was forced to submit to a great deal of inconvenience. Things went on like this for a short time, when I brought the matter before the Chapter, and also suggested that we should have a weekly bill made out, as in other cathedrals, and after a vast deal of trouble I gained this point, and the Chapter agreed to adopt my plan.

"One of the Canons, finding the head boy did not trot about the choir half the service-time as before, was very angry, so that during his residence the new arrangement had to be discontinued in order that he might have the pleasure of seeing the boy continue his perambulations.

"The names of the choir when I first went to Windsor were Mallar, Francis, Palmar, Jarman, Smith, West, French, Mitchell, Salmon, Hobbs, and Harris.

"Most of them were aged men, and not efficient; in fact, only four of them could sing, and I had not been at Windsor many months before Jarman, the alto, who was a very good singer, was down with consumption, which carried him off in a few months.

"The choir was by his death left with only one tenor and two basses efficient, and the services were dependent upon the boys and the three men above-mentioned. Unfortunately the tenor was in pecuniary difficulties, and was arrested. Thus the choir was reduced to two basses.

"The Dean at that time, and my predecessor, Mr. Skeats, did not get on well together. In consequence of matters being so unpleasant between them, two of the Canons (at this time there were twelve) sent for me, and gave me good advice how to act with regard to the said Dean. They told me that if I humoured him I should get on very well. This advice I acted upon with advantage, for being young I could submit to what an older man would not have done.

"At this time there was no procession into the Chapel, and the Dean used to take his seat in the stalls in order to save time.

"He would often send for me, and say, '"Deliver us this afternoon," I am going for a drive.' This 'Deliver us' was an exceedingly short anthem by Batten.

"During the time that I was on trial, I went into the Chapel to practise for a few minutes on the organ, and, having spoken a word to Tucker, the sexton, a very quaint character, who was employed in dusting the Chapel, he said, 'If I could play the organ like that, I wouldn't be here dusting!'

"When I was appointed organist he was asked who had received the post, and replied, 'They have appointed a boy.'

"At first he took a fancy to me, and was very

civil, a most unusual thing for him. But 'a change came o'er the spirit of the dream,' for finding the people stay after Chapel to hear the new organist, he feared they would see the cenotaph. This privilege he considered they ought to pay for, as in those days the sextons thought themselves the proprietors of the Chapel.

" On one occasion someone remarked to Tucker that the organ sounded very grand, and his reply was, ' I wish the organ would bust !'

" He was an extraordinary man in his way, pleasant enough out of Chapel, but when on duty he was a lion.

" Although a small man, he was very powerful, and he told me that with a Turk's head broom he had taken cobwebs off the roof of the Chapel. In his early days he was a servant of one of the Canons, as most of the officers of the Chapel have been. Once, when his master went out of residence, he walked to Egham, intending to take the long stage to Winchester. When the coach drove up, however, it was full, and Tucker made no more ado, but walked to his master's living, some distance below Winchester. On his arrival his master asked where he had come from, and when Tucker explained, very kindly ordered him refreshment, with a glass of brandy and water, and sent him to bed, thinking he must be quite knocked up.

" Notwithstanding his long walk, to everyone's surprise Tucker was the first up the next morning, just as if nothing had happened.

" Many years before I remember him he was on one occasion, walking up from Frogmore on the raised pathway, when whom should he meet but King George III., with Queen Charlotte and all the junior members of the royal family, who were then children.

" Tucker like a loyal Englishman jumped off the footpath into the road.

" The King stopped and asked him why he did so, and receiving no reply, said : ' You jumped off the pathway for your own pleasure, now jump on again for mine.'

" People entertained the idea that Tucker was a man of wealth, and accordingly two burglars entered his house one night.   He, although upwards of ninety years of age, jumped out of bed and captured one of them.

" Another character I well remember who was at St. George's when I was appointed, was a queer individual named Roach.   When I first knew him he was cloister-keeper, and in that capacity wore a glazed hat with the words 'Dean and Canons' on it.

" In a few months he became belfry-keeper. On his appointment to this post (which includes blowing the organ, digging the graves, etc.), I offered my congratulations to him, when he took hold of my arm and said, ' I tell you what, young man, whenever you wants wind you shall 'ave it.'

" The first Sunday after this appointment, just as I was finishing the voluntary, he shouted out, loud enough for everyone to hear, 'Done, sir ? ' at which unseemly conduct I was so shocked that I fled from the organ-loft as quickly as possible.

" On one occasion Roach was digging a grave for a military knight, and one of the old knights said to him, ' You are getting very full here, Roach.' Roach replied, ' I mean to have a whole row of you along here.'   Another time, after the organ was considerably enlarged by William IV., a friend went into the organ-loft and questioned Roach about the blowing of the instrument.   He replied, ' It's all very well for that young man to sit figuring there (meaning me), but it'll take the wind out of any man to blow the Hallelujah Chorus, I don't care what country he comes from.'

CHAPTER VII.

ONLY a few weeks before His Majesty's death, Mr. Elvey took his choir, by request, to the Castle, to perform selections from the " Messiah."

On every desk he placed a card, giving full directions for the performance, to avoid all confusion; thus showing, even at this early period, his great attention to detail.

One of these is still preserved as a relic by Mr. William Corden, who played the violin on this occasion.

Queen Adelaide was delighted with the music, and frequently beat time to it with her hands, but its effect on the King was so soothing, that he slept peacefully during the greater part of the performance. Shortly after, His Majesty presented his portrait to Elvey, a gift which was highly prized as a memento of his kind benefactor.

Both William IV. and Queen Adelaide had

always taken a great interest in St. George's Chapel.

Soon after the former came to the throne the Dean and Canons were allowed to return to their stalls, from which they had been ejected by George IV.

In some way or other they had offended His Majesty, and, said he, " I'll teach you to whom the Chapel belongs!" and from that day they were not allowed to sit in the seats they now occupy, until August 8th, 1830.

At 2 o'clock on the morning of June 20th, 1837, King William IV. passed away.

What a strange mingling of joy and sorrow this event caused! sorrow for the death of the kind and gentle King, sympathy with the widowed Queen, and joy for the accession of one who appeared then, and has since proved herself to be, so ably fitted for her exalted position.

The sadder side of this event was announced to Windsor and the neighbourhood by the solemn tolling of the bell in the Curfew Tower, about which the following somewhat amusing tale is related : Roach, the belfry - keeper previously alluded to, seems to have received a broad hint that the King was near his end, and waited about until he received the news that all was over, when with haste he repaired to the deanery, arousing the inmates by ringing the bell at the Cloister entrance with all his might and main.

It was useless for the butler to ask him, "What do you want here at this time of night?" His business was with the Dean, and no one else.

This distinguished person, aroused from his slumbers, and clad, not in his surplice, but in another garment which should be "always white," called from the top of the stairs:

"What is the matter, Roach?"

"Billy be dead.   Be I to ring the bell?"

"What Billy?"

"The King, to be sure."

"Oh! yes, Roach, you may toll the bell."

Thus was the news spread that the King was dead, and that the young Princess Victoria was queen.

Shortly after, the Heralds arrived in Windsor, and a procession was formed, which was joined by Elvey and his choir, preceded by the Dean and Canons in their robes.   Thus, in solemn state, they proclaimed Her Majesty Queen in various parts of the royal borough.

Then followed vast preparations for the funeral

of William IV., no expense being spared to give due honour to the deceased monarch.

Upon this occasion the whole nave of the chapel was raised on a level with the choir and carpeted, which has never since been done for any event. Everything was carried out with lavish splendour, and Sir George has said that it was the most gorgeous ceremonial he had ever witnessed.

The gay uniforms of the soldiers, and the magnificent dress of the various State officials, lit up by the flare of countless torches, presented a scene of marvellous grandeur, and made the spectators almost forget the solemnity of the occasion.

A few months after the Queen's accession, Mr. Elvey was appointed, by royal warrant, her organist at Windsor. Although this was a purely honorary post, he was never willingly absent from St. George's during the time the Court was at Windsor.

Being so young when he entered upon his duties, he found it at first somewhat difficult to bring the choir into subjection, but the experience he had had at Oxford helped him greatly, and by steady perseverance he gained his point.

One thing seems to have been a sore trouble to him. This was a litany that the choir for some time had been in the habit of rendering, and with which they were loath to part. He wrote to Dr. Crotch on the knotty question, and the correspondence is given below :

"Windsor Castle.

"SIR,

"I hope you will pardon my troubling you, but I am anxious to have your opinion upon a point upon which the choir of St. George's Chapel and myself differ. For the last few years a new litany of Soper's has been performed here, the melody of which runs thus :

"After having submitted to hear the above for some time (which was a GREAT *favourite*), I made an effort to introduce the old one of Tallis again, and I am happy to state I have succeeded; but I am sorry to add, the choir and myself differ in regard to the real way of performing the same.

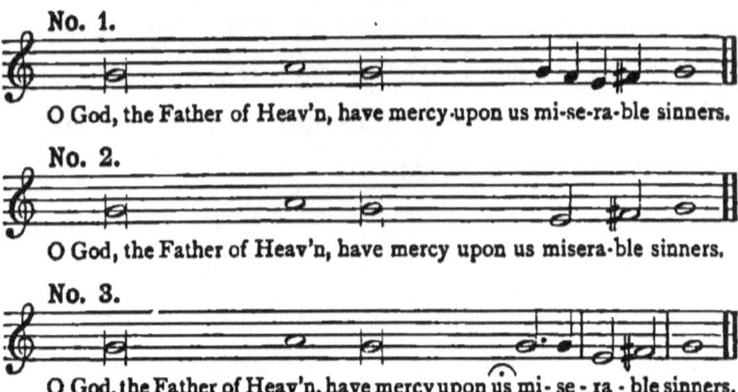

" The effect of No. 2 at the word 'miserable' is as follows :

" No. 3 is the way in which it is printed in Boyce, vol. i., and the melody is the same in the chanter's part as it is in the arrangement for the choir. I have, in the parts copied for the use of the choir, attended closely to the accent of the words as they are there expressed, but if in these modern days it should be altered, I certainly must see it done by an eminent musician, who I can look up to, before I can submit to any innovation made upon our good old church music.

" If, sir, you should sanction their mode in preference to Boyce, I will readily agree to the alteration you may suggest, whether it be in favour of Boyce or any other.

*   *   *   *   *

(Signed) " G. J. ELVEY."

Dr. Crotch sent the following reply :

" SIR,

"I decidedly prefer No. 3 to both the others. I should place the accent on '*us*,' but would not make a pause on the note. ' Upon ' should be short notes :

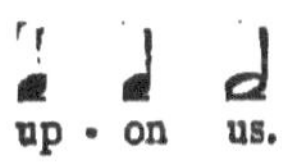

up · on us.

"I consider the litany in Boyce's collection not only better than others, but one of the finest pieces of ancient church music extant.

(Signed) " WM. CROTCH."

CHAPTER VIII.

DURING these early years the royal borough was the scene of much musical activity, and excellent concerts, under Mr. Elvey's direction, were constantly given by the Windsor and Eton Amateur Musical Society, the forerunner of the present Windsor and Eton Choral Society.

The Queen's Band included such noted musicians as Sainton, Cusins, John Day, Dr. Chipp (afterwards of Ely), Horatio Chipp, Hardy, Hill, Weist Hill, Anderson, Cramer, and members of the Griesbach and Harpur families. They constantly assisted Mr. Elvey at these concerts, so that then, and for many years, until the change of arrangements in the band, the Choral Society always had a splendid orchestra for its concerts, and was able to give better performances than have been possible at any time since.

Elvey, in his turn, would frequently, on special occasions, take his violin up to the Castle and play with the band. Many were the pleasant evenings these eminent musicians spent together, both on Sundays and other days.

One night the band-master, rather a choleric man, met with an unfortunate accident. Having put his violin down to reprimand some offender, in his excitement he suddenly stepped back, putting his foot right through the belly of his fiddle.

At this the band was convulsed with laughter, which continued to increase as he held it up, saying, nearly crying meanwhile :

"You wouldn't laugh if it were *your* fiddle."

In the summer of 1839, Elvey, tired of a solitary life, was happy in securing for himself a truly congenial partner in Harriet Skeats, the daughter of his predecessor. The wedding took place at St. George's, Hanover Square. His wife is described by all who knew her as being very pretty and charming in manner; indeed, none can speak warmly enough of her bright and happy disposition.

This union was a truly blessed one, for the young pair were not only congenial in their musical tastes, but their hearts were united on the all-important point of love to their Saviour.

Morning and evening Dr. Elvey called his household together for family worship; and delightful indeed it was to be present on these occasions to hear his devout and earnest reading and prayer. Truly God's blessing thus daily sought, no matter how busy he might be, was the reason of his success in all that he undertook. He always threw his whole soul into his work, and looking after every item of the arrangements himself, he spared neither time nor trouble to have everything as perfect as possible.

His life is a striking example of how a man occupying a most important public position, can, without unduly forcing his religious opinions upon others, yet let his light so shine before men that they can see his good works.

Reverence for everything that was good and great both in the past and the present intertwined and ennobled every part of his character, the beautiful features of which were, his childlike faith in God's word, his great humility, and the fact that, despite his natural timidity, he was fearless of consequences where duty was concerned.

Thus, when choosing boys or men for his choir, no wish to please friends or fear of offending them would influence his decision.

Indeed, in one instance at least he suffered for

many years much petty persecution from having declined an incompetent boy.

Duty throughout his life always took the first place, and, although frequently this exposed his keenly sensitive nature to intense pain, nothing would make him flinch.

In 1838, George Elvey obtained his Mus. Bac. degree, for which he wrote an oratorio, " The Resurrection and Ascension."

In April, 1840, by a special dispensation from the Duke of Wellington, then Chancellor of the University of Oxford, he was enabled to take his doctor's degree two years earlier than was allowed by the statutes. For this he composed his anthem, " The ways of Zion do mourn," which was cordially approved by Dr. Crotch, then Professor of Music at Oxford. On April 21st, before the degree was actually conferred, his anthem was performed in the music-room of Windsor Castle before the Queen, Prince Albert, the Duchess of Kent, and other distinguished persons.

The following account appeared at the time :

" On Tuesday morning last, previous to Her Majesty taking her usual exercise in the Park, she was graciously pleased to order the performance of Mr. Elvey's beautiful exercise for his

Mus. Doc. degree, and for this purpose Her Majesty's private band was in attendance to take the instrumental parts, and members of the Sacred Harmonic Society to support the choruses. We have had the opportunity of hearing and judging of this sublime piece of music. It was universally admired on its performance in Cardinal Wolsey's Chapel a few days since before a large company, and we are assured by a gentleman who was present that nothing could have gone off more to the satisfaction of all concerned, and not the least so to that of the composer himself.

" Her Majesty on the conclusion of the performance was graciously pleased to enter into conversation with Mr. Elvey, and spoke in the kindest and most encouraging manner to him, she herself being no mean judge of music. H.R.H. Prince Albert also complimented him on the production, and expressed his delight in having had an opportunity of hearing it.

" It gives us great pleasure to record such testimonials in favour of this ' exercise,' and the more so as the opinion of the first man of the age, Dr. Crotch, has stamped it with his approval, and thus has offered more than a guarantee for its originality and beauty."

In June the exercise was performed in the Music Room at Oxford.

Long before the arrival of the Vice-Chancellor the room was crowded to excess, and numbers were obliged to return without being able even to get near the door. Dr. Stephen Elvey, his brother, conducted in the magnificent crimson and white robes presented to him by his pupils when he took his doctor's degree.

The principal vocal parts were sung by members of the St. George's choir, and the chorus was given in splendid style by the choristers of New College, the lay-clerks of the Cathedral, and members of the Sacred Harmonic Society.

In the Oxford paper at the time occurs the following notice:

"To attempt to particularize where the whole was good would be useless. The anthem was one of the finest compositions it has been our lot to hear performed for a degree in music, and the unanimous applause it met with from a delighted audience confirmed the judgment that had selected Mr. Elvey as private organist to the Queen."

Delighted indeed was the elder brother, whom he loved so well, at the splendid name his almost son and pupil was making for himself.

Speaking of his organ-playing at this time, a gentleman writes:

"The organ at St. George's, Windsor, from its magnitude and quality of tone, gives him an opportunity of displaying the exuberance of his rich imaginative powers and scientific execution; while the chaste and solemn style in which the Cathedral service is performed reflects great credit upon his taste. Whatever musical honour may be conferred upon him will not be greater than he deserves, for Dr. George Elvey, though so young a man, ranks as one of the first performers on that noble instrument."

How delightful it is to his friends to hear this opinion confirmed fifty-three years afterwards! and we feel that our readers will pardon us for giving another quotation:

"The late Sir George Elvey, organist of St. George's Chapel, was considered among his compeers as the greatest master that ever touched the pedals during the present century."

How few young men at such an early age, or, indeed, much later, could have received such an amount of attention and praise without being in the least affected by it.

Such, however, was the case with Dr. Elvey.

He remained the same gentle, unobtrusive, humble-minded man to the close of his life.

Perhaps, indeed, it would have been better for him had he asserted himself a little more, and thus saved himself from the annoyance caused by people of inferior abilities, who not infrequently took advantage of this trait in his character to impose upon him.

On November 12th of this year, his oratorio, to which reference has been made as having been composed in 1838 for his Mus. Bac. degree, was performed by the Sacred Harmonic Society at Exeter Hall. The place was crammed, as the work, which was acknowledged to be a fine one, excited great interest in the musical world.

The following interesting account was given at the time :

" The performance opened with an anthem by the leader, Mr. Perry. This was followed by a short oratorio by Dr. Elvey, which appeared to be the principal attraction of the evening. The subject of it was ' The Resurrection and Ascension. Had Dr. Elvey failed in this effort, one of the most arduous that a musician can undertake, such a failure would have been by no means discreditable. But he has succeeded, and to such an extent as to give him a fair title to be ranked among that class to which Handel and Haydn belong. From the general feeling of the audience, and its effect on ourselves, we are led to predict that Dr. Elvey can, and will, produce works of the greatest power and effect.

"The reputation of Dr. Elvey as a profound musician and excellent organist must be greatly enhanced by this composition."

CHAPTER IX.

IN the winter of 1846 the Doctor started a music class at his house for the inhabitants of Windsor and Eton, which was greatly enjoyed by the members, who appear to have found the royal borough exceedingly dull in winter-time.

The class numbered thirty-five, and in a few weeks' time, under Dr. Elvey's careful instruction, the members were able to give a very good concert for the amusement of the poorer classes in the two towns. After one of these concerts, probably during a subsequent season, the following remarks appeared in the local paper :

" We have great pleasure in the concerts which our zealous and talented Dr. Elvey has instituted for the relief of the monotony of life in Windsor, and we have moreover much satisfaction in assuring him that the entertainment he offered on Wednesday night was very much admired by the crowded assembly which filled the Town Hall.

" His ' Mount Carmel ' was greatly appreciated.

He has, indeed, done much to entitle him to the grateful consideration of Windsor and Eton, by introducing a taste for the humanizing pleasure of his art, at the cost to himself of a great deal of time and labour.

" We know it to be the general feeling of the members of the Society that the evenings which he devotes to them during six months of the year are sources of pleasure and improvement to them.

" We know that he is repaid, as he deserves to be, by their unanimous sentiment of gratitude and esteem."

The reason for Dr. Elvey's oratorio, " Mount Carmel," mentioned above, remaining, to a great extent, a sealed book, is given by the composer himself. His oratorio had been written before Mendelssohn's " Elijah ;" they both treated of the same subject, and were very much on the same dramatic lines, but Dr. Elvey's conclusions on the subject were perfectly just. "What chance," he said, "would my work have against Mendelssohn's masterpiece? When ' Elijah' was produced at Birmingham it sounded the death-knell of ' Mount Carmel,' and cut the ground from under my feet. Mendelssohn's popularity put everything else in the shade, and my oratorio was overshadowed and crowded out."

This was a bitter disappointment to him, but with his ever-generous feelings to rivals, it was not permitted to interfere with his great admiration for Mendelssohn, whose " Lieder " he delighted in playing to the close of his life. He always spoke in warm praise of him, and Sir George's pianoforte pupils will remember how the celebrated " Lieder ohne Worte," and Stephen Heller's works of a like nature, were constantly resorted to for developing taste and expression.

It is quite true that the brothers Elvey had the correct reading of Handel's works, as regards tempo, etc., by tradition and instinct through Dr. Crotch, but they obtained their more modern ideas by personal contact with Bennett, Cipriani Potter, Moscheles, Mendelssohn, Thalberg, and Czerny.

When Mendelssohn paid his memorable visit to Windsor Castle, and played to the Queen and the Prince Consort, " I believe," says a friend, " that Dr. Elvey and he performed upon the Chapel organ, and that the former went to London, by invitation through the Horsleys, to hear Mendelssohn preside at the Exeter Hall instrument."

Sir George was a great admirer of Mendelssohn's pianoforte playing, and said he had only heard one other performer at all equal to him.

Miss Horsley frequently recited her great friend Mendelssohn's music upon Dr. Elvey's piano, so that he got the correct rendering of most of his well-known melodies.

Charles Horsley, on one of his many journeys to Windsor for the sake of the Sunday afternoon services at the Chapel, took the concluding voluntary, and, not being used to the F compass of the pedals, was not always sure of hitting the right note. His manual dexterity was manifest, but the strange pedal-board caused him much trouble.

An instrumental trio of Horsley's frequently found a place in the programmes of the musical gatherings held in Dr. Elvey's house.

Thalberg paid a visit to him, and played his fantasia on "Mosè in Egitto" in the drawing-room on the Broadwood Grand.

This was placed along a wall that divided the room from the dining-room, and the player sat almost in a corner, on the right-hand side of the fireplace. The sound being focussed into that particular spot in the room, it had often been noticed how very distinctly the harmonics of the bass notes could be detected.

When Thalberg sat down to play he hit by chance upon the lowest C, and this phenomenon so struck him that he left off in order to call attention to the fact of the manifest preponderance of the flat seventh in the harmonic series on that particular note C.

This led Dr. Elvey to have a wire string stretched upon a wooden frame to experiment upon, and the sound-board was marked at the proper distances to show how the harmonics were produced. As this became associated with Thalberg's visit, it created an additional interest in him and all his works.

This incident gave zest to the inventive powers of Dr. Elvey and his pupils, and finding how Crotch had printed minute directions as to the length in inches of a pendulum for determining the tempo of most of Handel's grand choruses and concertos, they set to work and attached a leaden weight to sundry yards of tape, with inch and half-inch measures carefully put down in ink, so that they might each have a home-made metronome at hand.

*   *   *   *   *

Elvey's next important composition was an Ode on the Birth of the Prince of Wales.

On Monday evening, December 14th, the Queen ordered a performance of this at the Castle, and a little before nine o'clock she entered the music-room, leaning on the arm of Prince Albert. The Duchess of Kent and a large party of guests were already assembled.

The ode was admirably performed by Her Majesty's private band, the choir of St. George's Chapel, and some members of the Exeter Hall Musical Society, conducted by Dr. Elvey.

After all was over, the Queen told Dr. Elvey how delighted she was with the music, and also expressed great pleasure at the way in which it was performed.

Prince Albert also afterwards sent for him, and in a very gracious manner thanked him for the performance.

The clergyman who wrote the ode was at one time curate of Windsor, and was a very eccentric character. He resided in a house on Thames Street Hill, where he successfully protected himself from too frequent visitors by keeping bees in his sitting-room and two fierce dogs outside.

He subsequently went out as chaplain to the Bishop of New Zealand, but he did not remain long abroad, and after his return the nervous excitement from which he had always suffered so increased that he was obliged to be placed under restraint.

He had a perfect passion for music, and was very fond of Dr. Elvey, whose organ-loft he loved to frequent.

On one 4th of June he escaped from confinement, and presented himself at his old friend's house in the Cloisters.

Naturally he was in a very excited state, and, upon being shown into the drawing-room, commenced walking rapidly to and fro, kicking a basket in front of him, to the great alarm of the inmates of the house.

Dr. Elvey, knowing the power music had over him, walked into the room, and, although considerably frightened to see the madman with a knife in his hand, quietly sat down to the piano and played all kinds of soothing melodies for some two hours. By this time his excited visitor had become perfectly tractable, and a carriage having arrived with a friend for whom Dr. Elvey had sent, the latter went up to him and said, very gently putting his hand on his arm, " Now, my friend, be persuaded and go back to your home."

At this, he allowed himself to be taken to the carriage, and went back without further trouble.

Dr. Elvey afterwards visited him at the Home, and, in response to pressing requests, gave the inmates some music, although the only instrument was what he extremely disliked—a harmonium. At last one man said : "Give us a Te Deum ? " and on Dr. Elvey's saying he thought that was rather a big order, he replied, to Elvey's intense amusement, "Well, then, give us a cut out of the middle."

*   *   *   *   *

The baptism of the infant Prince of Wales took place in St. George's Chapel on January 25th, 1842.

Dr. Elvey arranged the musical portion of the service for this, submitting the programme beforehand to H.R.H. Prince Albert.

The following letter was sent to him at the time, at the direction of the Prince :

" SIR,

"You will observe by these marks (made by the Prince himself) that the march in ' Judas ' is to be played before the service ; the ' Hallelujah

Chorus' after the service, and the overture to 'Esther' while the royal party is retiring.

"H.R.H. does not think that he will be able to attend the rehearsal on Monday.

"Your obedient servant,

(Signed) "CH. AHNUNG.

"Windsor Castle, *22nd*."

One of the choristers, young Foster, hearing that the Prince of Wales was to be christened in Jordan water, carefully secreted a small bottle in his jacket pocket. After the ceremony, seeing several ladies dipping their handkerchiefs in the font, he crept cautiously up when all seemed engaged in conversation, and, dropping *his* in, with one quick movement gave it a good soak, and, escaping from the Chapel, squeezed it into his bottle. This treasure he preserved for some time.

CHAPTER X.

THE Doctor, having now undertaken the cares of a household, found his means very straitened, as his stipend from the Chapter was at this time only £135, and his constant attendance at the Chapel, and many other duties, interfered greatly with his time for teaching. He therefore petitioned the Chapter to increase his salary, but this they appeared unwilling to do, although the revenues of the Chapel at that time were very large.

Dr. Elvey therefore sent in an application for Exeter Cathedral, which was then in want of an organist, and proceeded there by coach to compete for the post, which he won.

On this occasion, as on the previous one when he competed at Windsor, he received many excellent testimonials—one, to which he attached especial value, being from the late Bishop Selwyn to this effect :

" He will not only discharge the duties of such a situation in a merely formal and devout manner, but he will do his utmost in his particular department to add to the solemnity and devotion of the Church Service.

(Signed) " G. A. NEW ZEALAND."

The trial took place just before Dr. Selwyn went out to New Zealand, and he has left on record the great pleasure he experienced in listening to Dr. Elvey's rendering of his favourite anthems.

The Dean and Chapter of Windsor, fearing at last that they would lose their gifted organist, agreed to give him the munificent (! ! !) sum of £200 per annum, and during the whole of his forty-seven years' service he was never offered any increase.

Indeed, he used to say that such was the humiliation attendant on his first and only petition, that nothing would have induced him to again approach the authorities.

Writing to an old pupil in 1869, Dr. Elvey speaks thus with regard to the much-sought-after post of cathedral organist :

" I quite agree with you in what you say about the position of a cathedral organist. It is one coveted by young musicians, but it is by no means a prize.

" I believe many parish organists are better off than those of the cathedrals."

In 1843, the Chapel organ was rebuilt and considerably enlarged, under Dr. Elvey's direction, and he at the time gave the following account of it to Mr. Thomas Willement, Fellow of the Society of Antiquaries, who published a book on the restoration of St. George's :

" This instrument of exquisite tone and great power was built by Green in the year 1790, and, though in daily use, it received but little repair, and no alteration from that period up to 1835. In this year, however, several additions were made to it by the command and at the private expense of his late majesty, William IV., consisting, amongst others, of the extension of the swell to tenor C, and the addition of double diapason pedal-pipes. But it has been during the past year that this instrument has received the greatest improvements, and become, under the hands of Messrs. Gray and Davison of London, fully worthy of the beautiful chapel in which it stands.

" The swell organ now extends to FF, and six new stops are added to it : sesquialtera, fifteenth, cornopean, clarion, hautboy, and double diapason. The swell of this organ is probably the most

perfect in the kingdom ; the unusual thickness of
the box and the improved principle of the shutters
enable the organist, from a scarcely audible sound,
to arrive at the full swell by the most gradual increase—an effect not to be attained by the swell as
usually constructed.

" The choir-organ has also been greatly improved by the introduction of a new stop, the
keraulophon, the recent discovery of Mr. Gray.
This delightful stop, whilst it resembles the reed
in its tone, has this great advantage, that it is not
subject, like it, to be out of tune—an advantage of
immense value in a solo stop, and more especially
in one so admirably suited as the keraulophon is
for an accompaniment to the voice.

" Great improvements have also been made to
the pedals, which now extend to F ; whilst, by the
addition of two octaves of unison pedal-pipes, the
power of the double diapason is greatly increased,
and a beautiful and effective light accompaniment
to the swell and choir-organ is obtained.

" Such, indeed, is the compass of the pedal, that
the difficult fugues of the great Sebastian Bach can
now be executed with ease.

" To the great organ new reed-stops have also
been added, and the large wooden false pipes,

which formerly were placed on the exterior of the organ case, have been removed, and metal pipes of the lower octave of the open diapason substituted in their room.

"The following is a list of the stops now contained in this instrument, thirty-seven in number :

SWELL ORGAN.

Double diapason.	Dulciana principal.	Cornopean.
Open diapason.	Principal.	Hautboy.
Stopped diapason.	Fifteenth.	Trumpet.
Dulciana.	Sesquialtera (three ranks).	Clarion.

GREAT ORGAN.

Open diapason, nave front.	Principal.	Mixture (two ranks).
Open diapason, choir front.	Twelfth.	Trumpet bass.
Stopped diapason.	Fifteenth.	Trumpet treble.
Clarabella flute.	Sesquialtera (three ranks).	Clarion.

CHOIR ORGAN.

Dulciana.	Principal.	Keraulophon.	Clarionet.
Stopped diapason.	Octave flute.	Bassoon.	

PEDAL ORGAN.

Double open diapason.	Open diapason.

COUPLERS.

Swell to great manual.	Swell manual to pedals.
Great manual to pedals.	Choir manual to pedals."

Foremost among his illustrious pupils at this period was H.R.H. the Prince Consort, who, always anxious to improve himself in every branch of art, took lessons in harmony from him, and at this time composed his celebrated Te Deum, etc.

The Prince, desiring to have the same performed, Dr. Elvey, ever anxious to give pleasure, conceived the idea of instrumenting the fine work for the band, and, rising early in the morning of the day it was to be performed, he not even allowed himself time to complete his toilette, but sat all day in his dressing-gown, working hard at arranging and copying the parts for the respective instruments, until it was time for him to prepare for the performance.

The Prince, always most kind and gracious to him, was delighted with his clever work, and expressed himself so warmly about it that Elvey felt well repaid for all the trouble he had taken.

This Te Deum, with Dr. Elvey's accompaniments, was used at the Jubilee service in Westminster Abbey.

A short time after the Prince sent him a pair of splendid silver candlesticks in remembrance of the occasion.

The Doctor took a great interest in the arrangements for the erection of an organ in the Park Church, with which he rendered the Prince Consort considerable assistance.

When the instrument was ready for use, the latter took Dr. Elvey over with him to try it, but directly the Doctor commenced to play the most unearthly sounds proceeded from under the organ-stool, much to their consternation.

It was then discovered that a little pet dog of the Doctor's had secreted himself in the carriage unobserved, and followed them into the Chapel.

At this period the Doctor was in very poor health, and by the advice of a physician whom he consulted, he adopted for some time the plan of taking a long walk as soon as he rose, and then returning home for bath and breakfast, which *régime* he found most beneficial.

Upon one of these early morning excursions he was exceedingly interested to see the French King, Louis Philippe, then on a visit to Her Majesty the Queen, likewise taking an early morning constitutional, and, what attracted his attention still more, was to see him walk up to one of the sentries, asking him something, which the man, not knowing by whom he was being addressed, was evidently unwilling to do, until a few words, quietly spoken, apprized him of the rank of his questioner.

Learning this, he at once acceded to the request made to him, and unfastening his knapsack, laid it on the ground and exhibited the whole contents to the King, who seemed most anxious to know with what kit the English soldiers were provided.

CHAPTER XI.

FROM the time he went to Windsor, until his retirement in 1882, Dr. Elvey was ever ready to help forward any scheme for the benefit of the royal borough.

In this way the Choral Society (which he started quite at the outset of his Windsor career), and, later on, the Madrigal Society, both owed much to his energy and ability.

Of course the posts he held in connection with these societies were purely honorary; but, far from suffering from this fact, his work for them was rendered conspicuous by a zeal and energy that no monetary recompense could have repaid.

He worked incessantly at the practices, regularly taking them himself, and doing all in his power to render the members thoroughly efficient.

But before this was achieved, many amusing incidents occurred. Occasionally a violinist, waxing warm at his work and forgetful of time, would arrive at the end of a movement whilst the others were yet in the middle.

One night, when practising " The Creation," the confusion at first was so great that the Doctor remarked laughingly to the members : " You have succeeded in depicting chaos better than Haydn ever intended."

In the early days of the Choral Society concerts were given alternately in the Mathematical School at Eton and the Windsor Town Hall. This hall stands in the High Street, and was built by Sir Christopher Wren. The large Banqueting Room and Justice Chamber, supported by stone pillars placed round the outer sides, give it the appearance of a Noah's Ark on stilts, or a colossal centipede similarly equipped.

The burgesses, fearing for their august persons, lest they should find themselves on the flags below one fine night, after or during a dance or some other festive gathering, requested the illustrious architect to place equally strong pillars in the centre as a measure of precaution. Failing to satisfy these good men and their merry wives that the structure was perfectly safe as he designed it, he reluctantly consented to set up pillars in the required position; but he privately ordered them to be made four inches shorter than the real supports.

Generations of happy aldermen lived and died in ignorance of this fact till the ceiling of the yard below had to be repaired, when the workmen discovered that the centre uprights had never touched the beams on which the rooms rested !

In this Banqueting Hall the concerts were held, and the Council Chamber was turned into an artistes' room.

The members of the Queen's private band were generally the principal instrumentalists ; at other times the bands of the regiments quartered in Windsor were engaged.

More often, contingents from each were requisitioned.

For many years no London principals were engaged for these concerts, and the members of the St. George's choir, men and boys, were the chief vocalists.

Sometimes they sang gratuitously, and sometimes received a guinea fee. For this they were derisively styled " guinea-pigs." At the first concerts of the season, oratorios were sometimes given entire; then, at a second, a cantata as an introduction to a miscellaneous latter half. At

these solos were fired off, and budding geniuses
came to the fore with new compositions or arrangements.   The Guards' bands were so accustomed
to play in the open air that it required much tact
and firmness on the part of the conductor to keep
these gentlemen within bounds, or the brass would
have overpowered the other parts of the orchestra.

Winterbottom, a subaltern to Tutton, bandmaster
to the Blues, composed a " March " with a high-
sounding title like the celebrated piece called
" The Battle of Prague."   It was descriptive of
the tramp to the fight, storming the citadel, the
chance shots, and lastly, the triumph of victory.
Unlike the ancient pianoforte solo the " cries of
the wounded " were left out.

The Foot-Guards with their side drums assisted
their Life-Guard friends to beat the introductory
roll-call, and a very considerable din they made
with their combined forces ; enough, indeed, to
unnerve the strongest yeoman, let alone the old
ladies of the royal borough.

As the movements followed one after another,
the sound waxed louder and more loud, till, as
one who was present says :

" We thought our ears would give way under
the strain, or the roof lift bodily, so as to let off

the tremendous volume of noise cooped up in so small a space."

The audience bore this for a time in abject terror, in the hope that after the storm would come the longed-for calm. But instead, excitement added more and more to their powers of execution, till the band seemed possessed of a maddened frenzy.

Some of the most timid amongst the listeners had moved to the door soon after the tempest of sound commenced, and the exodus went on until the Town Hall was wellnigh empty, and the orchestra was allowed to blow itself off.

When at length the finale came, Dr. Elvey shouted his loudest "Bravo!" from the safe distance of the Council Chamber, "Bravo, Winterbottom! you have fairly vanquished the foe; and played them all out!"

Quite unconscious of his surroundings, Winterbottom looked very crestfallen, and retired from the conductor's desk, wiping his face, a sadder, but a wiser man.

The following extract from a letter written to a friend by Sir George Elvey respecting the drums belonging to the Choral Society, may not be out of place here.

"Dear ———,

"Keeton has asked me about the drums belonging to the Choral Society. . . . General Reid gave them to the society through me, and I purchased them of a Mr. Potter, who had a shop near Westminster Bridge. . . . I was told at the time that they were used at Vauxhall Gardens in the time of Handel.

"They are very fine drums, and used to cover a multitude of sins. . . ."

A further page in the history of these drums may be inserted here. In after years the Choral Society became bankrupt, and all its possessions were put up for sale. Dr. Elvey bought the drums to save them, but allowed the society to continue to use them as before.

The General Reid above-mentioned was a good friend to the Choral Society, for not only did he originally present the drums, but the whole of the orchestra, including the fittings and the chandeliers above the platform.

These chandeliers were telescoped, so that they might be pushed up out of the way of those performing upon the orchestra.

Besides the concerts that Dr. Elvey got up

with the Choral Society, he had many private musical entertainments at his own house.

Many interesting programmes of part-music were gone through in this way by the choir; and these alternated with more varied entertainments, at which trios and quartettes were played.

As a specimen of these, two programmes are given below:

Friday Evening, February 2nd, 1849.

SYMPHONY—PIANO, VIOLIN, VIOLONCELLO—*Haydn.*
MADRIGAL—" Merrily wake music's measure "—*Barnett.*
GLEE—" By Celia's arbour "—*Horsley.*
SONG—*Mr. Lockey.*
MADRIGAL—" Gather ye rosebuds "—*G. J. Elvey.*
DUET—" What are the wild waves saying ? "—*Glover.*
GLEE—" Spring's delights "—*Müller.*
MADRIGAL—" Lo, the bee "—*Balfe.*
GLEE—" When winds breathe soft "—*Webbe.*
SONG—*Mr. Lockey.*
GLEE—" Mark'd you her eye ? "—*Spofforth.*
SYMPHONY IN D, PIANO, VIOLIN, VIOLONCELLO—*Beethoven.*
MADRIGAL—" Flora gave me fairest flowers "—*Wilbye.*
GLEE—" With sighs, sweet rose "—*Callcott.*
CATCH—" They say there is an echo here "—*Herschell.*
SOLO VIOLONCELLO—*H. Chipp.*
MADRIGAL—" Down in a flow'ry vale "—*Festa.*
The Waits.

" The following pieces will be performed by the choristers of St. George's Chapel, Windsor, with

the permission of Dr. Elvey, and assisted by his
pupils.

PART FIRST.

OVERTURE—"Caliph of Bagdad "—*Boieldieu.*
GLEE—" The Chough and Crow "—*Bishop.*
MADRIGAL—" Away, thou shalt not love me "— *Wilbye,* 1598.
DUET—" Murmuring sea "—*Glover.*
SONG—" We're a' noddin' "—*Hawes.*
GLEE—" When shall we three meet again ? "—*Horsley.*
MADRIGAL—" Fly aloft "— *Wilbye.*
GLEE—" Strike the harp "—*Stevens.*
LAUGHING TRIO—" Va Dasi via Di qua "—*Martini.*

PART SECOND.

FANTASIA—Airs from " Norma "—*Bellini.* •
GLEE—" Blow, gentle gales "—*Bishop.*
MADRIGAL—" Now is the month of maying "—*Morley.*
SONG—" Sweet years of youth "—*Linter.*
SOLO AND CHORUS—"Come unto these yellow sands "—*Purcell.*
ROUND—" Wind, gentle evergreen "—*Hayes.*
SONG—" Where the bee sucks "—*Dr. Arne.*
MADRIGAL—" Down in a flow'ry vale "—*Festa.*
SOLO VIOLONCELLO.
TRIO—" Full of doubt and full of fear "—*Bishop.*
God Save the Queen."

Once a year the choristers prepared a play;
this was also performed in Dr. Elvey's drawing-
room.

These performances were a source of great

pleasure to all his friends in Windsor and the neighbourhood, and by this means a taste for good music was steadily cultivated in Windsor. Speaking of the choristers reminds one that at this period they had a somewhat remarkable man, Josiah French, for their schoolmaster.

He was one of the two good basses described by Dr. Elvey as being in the choir when he went to Windsor. This man was greatly respected by everyone—and more especially by the boys—for he did not believe in spoiling the child by sparing the rod. French was of artistic tastes; his walls were covered with oil-paintings, not only in the rooms, but in the passages, landings, and stairs, from hall to garret.

He was a keen collector of *objets d'art* and the happy possessor of a gold-headed malacca cane with which King George III. used to walk about Windsor.

Bristow, the artist, a constant visitor at his house, having supplied every nook and corner with almost living specimens of his art, was occupied in filling up the panels and doors with his inventive genius. At this time a pet dog belonging to the wife of one of the Eton masters died, and she sent for Bristow in order to keep in memory the departed animal by having it included in a picture. Bristow did not care for the job, but having the offer of good terms, he reluctantly consented to carry out the work.

When the oil-painting was delivered, the likeness of the dead favourite did not answer the lady's expectations. At an interview, the artist having been paid his fee according to agreement, she suggested certain alterations of which he did not approve ; but to satisfy her he took away the picture, which was returned to its owner a few days later, with a tin pot tied to a string added to the tail of the dog.

No amount of entreaty would induce Bristow to touch the canvas again.

During the visit of the Emperor Napoleon to the Queen at Windsor in 1853, a rather amusing incident occurred.

The day after his arrival Dr. Elvey and a pupil were on their way to afternoon service at the Chapel, when they were astonished to see Mr. French (who, by the bye, was an enthusiastic autograph hunter) running down the hill from the Castle towards them, his hat off in one hand, the other waving a piece of paper above his head in the most frantic manner, all the time shouting at the top of his voice, "I've got it. I've got it." In answer to Dr. Elvey's anxious inquiry, "What have you got?" he gasped out at last, between struggles for breath, "Why, the Emperor's autograph, to be sure."

A short period after this, poor French was leaving his house to attend service at the Chapel, when, turning back for something he had forgotten, he dropped into a chair, and died in a moment, from disease of the heart. He left no will, and all his valuable collections were sold, including the aforesaid gold-headed stick, which was bought by Mr. Lockey, and duly flourished whenever he came to Windsor.

By the way, Mr. Lockey was for a few years a lay-clerk in the St. George's choir. He was a very fine singer, and all who heard him felt that his provincial fame would soon reach the ears of the London *entrepreneurs;* and, once heard at Exeter Hall, his success as the leading tenor in sacred music was assured. He had the crowning distinction of singing the tenor music in "Elijah" at a first performance of that oratorio in Birmingham in 1846, and winning the gratitude of Mendelssohn himself. Curiously enough, the two happened to be walking together in the High Street at Oxford when the tidings of Elvey's appointment at St. George's Chapel reached the city.

Dr. Elvey wrote very effective anthems to show off the rare excellence of Lockey, and Foster, then a celebrated boy in the choir ; these his modesty has withheld from publication.

Foster, who is now an alto in Westminster Abbey, still speaks with much affection of his old master, and of the excellent musical education he gave him.

Elvey trained all his choristers to read music accurately, and this boy was especially noted. When Mendelssohn first produced " St. Paul," the Prince Consort sent down to ask the Doctor to bring up " little Foster " to the Castle to sing over parts of the new oratorio to the Queen and himself.

Among other pieces, Foster sang " Jerusalem " and " I will sing of Thy great mercies."

Her Majesty was so pleased with his performance, that, at the close, she crossed the room and patted him approvingly on the head.

CHAPTER XII.

EARLY in December of the year 1849, Queen Adelaide died at Stanmore Priory. She had always taken a keen interest in Elvey and his work at the Chapel, attending the service there on every opportunity when she was in Windsor.

When any member of the royal family died, it was, and is still, the custom that all the keys of the Chapel, those of the organ-loft and organ included, should be handed to the Lord Chamberlain, pending the making of arrangements for the funeral.

Usually, Sir George Smart, organist of the Chapel Royal, St. James's, came down to Windsor to preside on these occasions. When Queen Adelaide died, Sir George Elvey, who had always felt his deposition to be a slight, acting on the advice of Lord Wriothesley Russell, drove to Stanmore Priory, and represented to the authorities the interest the late Queen Dowager had always taken in the music at the Chapel. He was sure it would have been her wish for him to play at her funeral, and he ultimately gained his point. He was enabled to make the necessary arrangements himself, and thenceforth presided at his own organ at all State ceremonials.

His happy home life was not unmixed with sorrow ; for his wife, always fragile and delicate, was during the latter years of her life a source of great anxiety and care. Together they passed through the sorrow of losing, one after another, many bright little lives which had come to gladden their home. It seemed as if the children, inheriting their mother's delicate constitution, could not, even with the loving care of a devoted father and mother and a faithful nurse, take sufficient hold on life to rise superior to the ordinary illnesses incidental to the most carefully nurtured childhood. One only, his father's namesake, survived—a puny, white-faced boy, a hothouse plant, reared with much tenderness and judicious care.

Mr. C. J. Verrinder, Mus. Doc., a pupil of Sir George's, and now organist at St. Mary's, West Kensington, says:

" My first relations with Master George, my master's son, were rather unfortunate.

" He was a big boy, long and thin, when I was introduced to the domestic circle. No one ever said nay to the son and heir for fear of offending the father and mother, for he was the very apple of their eye. He had never been allowed to have companions or play rough games, but one fine morning he brought his whip-top into my practice room, where I was playing, and began to make a noise at my back, as I sat with my face to the piano.

" I called to him to stop, but he was not to be thwarted; so quickly jumping off my perch, I gave him to understand that I would not have it. He immediately lashed my legs with the whip. I had been launched upon the sea of life at eight years of age, and had had the usual cuffs from senior boys, canings from masters, etc., but, at the age of thirteen, when smarting under cuts administered by a younger boy, you do not stop to think whether the lashes are dealt by your master's son or anyone else; so, regardless of consequences, I soundly boxed Master George's ears, and bundled him out of the room, howling, you may be sure.

" For this I was severely reprimanded by Mrs. Elvey, who quickly appeared on the scene, followed by cook, parlour-maid, and faithful Ellen, who stood aghast at my audacity.

" I defied all female interference, and was left

severely alone. However, when Master George discovered that I was not to be trifled with, we became warm friends. I taught him how to sail boats, spin tops, and other boyish tricks. I licked his dog into shape as well, and much amused was the Doctor to see this animal and his funny ways.

"Years after, when I went up to Oxford for my Mus. Bac. degree, I visited George Elvey at his rooms at New College, and became a member of the same old place."

*   *   *   *   *

Of the high quality of the choir of St. George's during Dr. Elvey's period there is no question. A well-known musician relates how he once sat up with him in the organ-loft during service. The Psalms were started with organ as usual, and no sooner had this been done than he exclaimed, " I have forgotten my keys; I must go and fetch them." He started off, the choir singing on. In due time he returned to the organ, and tried, with a soft stop, to see if his singers had dropped in pitch. They were dead in tune, and the accompaniment was taken up. A better proof of training could hardly be given.

This test of their powers, Dr. Verrinder, one of

his pupils, says, far from being an isolated case, was of frequent occurrence.

When asked " How did you choose boys ? " he replied on one occasion, " I like to hear a boy sing something—a song, for instance. I could tell at once from this if he had the making of a chorister in him. You cannot give boys musical talent, and the organist often has a trying task in endeavouring to do it."

Sir George, in his later years, used to relate some amusing incidents that took place when he was selecting choristers.

One was of a boy very strongly recommended to him from Wales, with what was supposed to be a very remarkable voice. This it certainly was, for the boy was really a young man, and Sir George would tell with much amusement how he was thoroughly alarmed when, the upper notes being attempted, the candidate turned nearly black in the face with the effort.

He was advised for the future to be content with his natural voice, and not to put himself to such a painful strain. This advice he owned to having received from others.

Another tale was of a boy who came with his parents from some remote country place, the whole party dressed in such extraordinary costumes that they looked as if they were travelling mountebanks. Upon hearing the boy sing, and the result being anything but satisfactory, his mother, as an excuse, remarked, " The Jews could not sing the Lord's song in a strange land."

She evidently did not wish to part with her son, for nothing could exceed her joy when Dr. Elvey told her that he did not think her boy would be of any use for St. George's.

Once a tall soldïer appeared at his house with his little son, having come a considerable distance in the hope of the child's being elected to fill the vacancy in the choir.

Dr. Elvey at once took them into his drawing-room, and endeavoured to test the child's voice, but not a sound would the little rascal utter, in spite of various promises of buns, etc., made to him by his father, added to piteous descriptions of his mother's grief when he should return.

At the first opportunity he dashed out of the room, and began kicking at the front door with all his might and main.

It is impossible to say what might have occurred had not one of the servants come out and checked the disturbance.

It was certainly ludicrous to see a man of six feet utterly baulked by a child of seven or eight years old.

At that period, and indeed till 1867, the same men and boys served Eton College as well as the Royal Chapel, and, with the one exception of Durham, they were better paid than any other choir, and had the advantage of being within thirty minutes of London.

During this time Dr. Elvey was constantly called upon to preside at the College organ ; in fact, on all important occasions his assistance was asked for, and readily granted.

At the opening of the new instrument a whole octave of services was held, with Dr. Elvey as accompanist.

THE OLD HORSE-SHOE CLOISTERS, WINDSOR.

From a photograph by Hills and Saunders.

CHAPTER XIII.

ON weekday mornings the music at St. George's was mostly selected from Boyce, Greene, and Croft's collections, frequently unaccompanied, and Dr. Verrinder says : " I confess I have never heard the compositions of Gibbons, Purcell, Blow, etc., given with so much artistic and devotional feeling as in the old days at the Chapel.

" The organ accompaniments to the Psalms were a thing to hear and not forget."

Mr. E. H. Thorne, who was also his pupil, says, " His style of organ-playing was pre-eminently a grand Church style, while his reading of many of the anthems of Croft, Boyce, Greene, and others was most striking, and instinct with religious, dramatic, and poetic feeling."

While the Metropolitan Church and Abbey were in a cold and languishing state about the middle of the century, St. George's Chapel possessed the finest and best-trained choir in England. On Sunday afternoons people flocked from all parts to hear as good a rendering of modern Church music as can now be heard in St. Paul's Cathedral, the organ being frequently supplemented by instrumentalists from the Queen's and Guards' bands.

After the Sunday services the tea-parties at the Elveys' house were great functions.

Always hospitable, on these occasions they kept open house, and friends from a distance were always most welcome.

Frequently the drawing-room was filled with visitors, among whom were whole families of Arbuthnots, Wrenches, Whitbreads, etc., etc. ; also Mrs. Smythe, whose daughter afterwards married Marshal Canrobert.

What a crowd of memories flit before one's mental vision when one thinks of those who used to meet in Dr. Elvey's drawing-room. Here originated the Choir Benevolent Fund Society. Grey, Lockey, and Shoubridge were wont to meet frequently to discuss and develop the scheme, and few festivals were more successful than the first one he'd in St. George's Chapel. Sir Frederick Ouseley used to rest in that room after playing extempore fugues on the Chapel organ, or Handel's chorus, " Fix't in His everlasting seat," over which

he would get so excited that he has been known
to break off before the end from sheer exhaustion
and inability to execute the music at the pace he
had worked up to.

And what a magnificent view there is from the
windows of that drawing-room! Cliefden, formerly the Duke of Westminster's seat on the
Thames, which one Sunday night the Doctor and
his friends watched in flames; Eton College, near
at hand; and Stoke Pogis Church, nestled among
the trees afar off—these are sights that, if once
seen, will never be forgotten.

How many are left who used to assemble in
the room high up on the wall above Thames
Street, and can bring back as photographs happy
recollections of the past?

One great friend of the Doctor's at this time,
whom we have omitted to mention, is the Hon.
Captain Bertie, his acquaintance with whom dated
from his Oxford days.

Captain Bertie was an officer in the Blues; he
acquired a taste for the organ at Oxford, and was
a diligent pupil of Dr. Stephen Elvey's, with whom
he studied. He collected a large number of the
works of the best masters, and also bought up and
preserved many manuscripts left by Dr. Crotch,

Professor of Music at the university, whose pupil he had been. He fully shared with the brothers Elvey their spirit of enthusiastic admiration for that great lecturer and contrapuntist.

When Captain Bertie came to Windsor with his regiment, he always called upon his old friend, with whom he ever enjoyed a chat; and, on Sunday afternoons, the concluding voluntary was usually played as a duet, the gallant captain taking the upper part, and Dr. Elvey the bass and pedals.

" Let Sinai tell," from Crotch's " Palestine," and the overtures and choruses from Handel's oratorios were favourite selections on these occasions.

The Captain, being a very small man, and also near-sighted, there was always a great struggle to keep him well-balanced on the organ stool. He kept his nose so close to the book that there was much difficulty in turning over for him, and as for changing from one manual to another, it was positively neck-breaking. Generally, during that operation, he would lose his place, if not his balance, and one or other of Dr. Elvey's pupils had to pick him up, both literally and figuratively. For this service the requital was generally a half-sovereign.

At the Spital barracks Captain Bertie had in his quarters a very fine grand pianoforte, by Broadwood. Whether this was an annoyance to some of the younger officers, or his love for music preventing his joining in their sports or pastimes irritated them, it is impossible to say, but these gentlemen, during the Captain's absence, smashed every string. It cost a considerable sum to replace them and repair the damage, but the event soon blew over.

When, after the little war with China, an envoy had to negotiate the terms of peace, Captain Bertie joined the staff.

Before setting sail for the Celestial Empire he informed Dr. Elvey that he had made his will, and left him his library and manuscripts.

The Captain was not long after attacked with yellow fever, from which he died.

In due course the large packing-cases of music, etc., arrived at Windsor, and Dr. Elvey became possessed of a most valuable addition to his library.

CHAPTER XIV.

ANOTHER gentleman who was a friend of the Doctor's for very many years was Mr. Tuckerman, the son of a rich merchant in America. He was a fair organist in his way, and had some knowledge of music. He came over to England armed with good letters of introduction, with the avowed object of collecting music and information (his ultimate intention being to found a library in New York), and to make himself acquainted with English form and mannerism, more especially in connection with Cathedral music, of which the Americans had a very imperfect knowledge. Thus began a friendship with Dr. Elvey, which lasted until Dr. Tuckerman's death in 1892.

Mr. Tuckerman's plan was to get letters to the organist of each cathedral in turn—say Durham, York, Chester, etc.—and to settle down in each city for one, two, or three months, as the case might be, make observations and copious notes,

and collect books on music, etc., then to start off
with these to his native land, deposit his treasures,
and give a series of musical lectures. These
finished, he would return to this side of the
Atlantic, take another district, and go through
the same process.

After two or three of these visits it was thought
by his compatriots that his efforts on behalf of the
advancement of music in his own country would
be very much enhanced if his hands could be
strengthened with the title and diploma of Doctor
of Music. Elvey, and several other eminent
cathedral organists, etc., drew up a petition, and
sent it, with some of Tuckerman's compositions,
to the then Archbishop of Canterbury, who granted
their prayer, and conferred upon him the much-
coveted distinction.

In due course Dr. Tuckerman expressed a wish
to go to Winchester, where Wesley, a notedly
eccentric man, was organist.

Wesley entertained far from friendly feelings
for Dr. Elvey, as he had never forgiven him, as
we have remarked previously, for the double defeat
he had received at his hands.

However, Dr. Elvey wrote him a letter, and,
armed with this, our American friend presented

himself at Wesley's door, and was ushered into the drawing-room.

On the appearance of the great man, Dr. Tuckerman, by way of breaking ground, ventured to say where he had come from, stated the object and purpose of his visit, and wound up by producing the letter from Dr. Elvey, which he handed to the friend (?) to whom it was addressed.

Wesley tore open the epistle, read it, and then threw it into the fire behind him, exclaiming, " Elvey! Who is Elvey ? "

Whereupon he rang the bell violently. The manservant, rushing in with great haste, his master addressed him in loud and distinct tones that were quite unmistakable: " John, this man is an impostor. Show him the door ! "

This operation was duly performed, and Dr. Tuckerman's feelings may be better imagined than described. He drove to the station forthwith, and making his way back to Windsor, presented himself to the Doctor, and explained, in no measured terms, the sort of reception he had met with at Winchester.

He had been ready to make allowance for little eccentricities, but for such behaviour he was wholly unprepared.

Dr. Elvey made the best excuse he could, and the subject was allowed to drop, but not without leaving a most uncomfortable impression.

On the Saturday fortnight after this gentleman had made his unfortunate pilgrimage to Winchester, a telegram was put into Elvey's hands, which ran thus : "Send down your friend Tuckerman ; I have put up ' The Wilderness ' for him to hear to-morrow."

Mr. Verrinder was at once sent off to Park Street with this missive, and on his return with Dr. Tuckerman to the Cloisters, the first question the latter asked was, "What shall I do ? " Elvey replied, " I don't like to urge too much upon you after your recent experience, but if you take my advice you will go. But telegraph an answer."

Tuckerman went by an afternoon train. Dr. Wesley met him at the railway station, and lodged him courteously in his house. After dinner they went into the Cathedral, and for two hours Wesley played the organ in his best manner, chiefly extempore.

On Sunday morning, Wesley in E was the service ; at evensong the anthem was " The Wilderness," played as Wesley alone could play it. When Dr. Tuckerman returned to Windsor on Monday evening, he said he had most thoroughly enjoyed his visit.

In connection with this anthem the following *bonmot* is recorded of Dr. Stephen Elvey.

He and Wesley were discussing some knotty point with considerable warmth, and at length Wesley, finding that he was getting the worst of the argument, exclaimed, " Elvey, you're a bear; I won't talk to you any longer."

To which Dr. Stephen promptly rejoined, "Well, if I am, I won't growl in your ' Wilderness.' "

Another friend of this period wrote the following account after Sir George's death :

" Truly do I myself feel the loss of Sir George, for whom I have cherished an almost lifelong affection. I shall never forget my first introduction to him, and can never cease to feel deeply grateful for all his kindness to me. It was in February, 1847, that I first came under his influence. I was tutor to the sons of Lord Wriothesley Russell, who was then in residence, and had frequent opportunities of hearing the Doctor's beautiful organ accompaniments at the services in St. George's. One afternoon, just as we were finishing our lessons, Lord Russell came, and, with a very kind remark, said that if I would accept them, he should be very glad to give me ten lessons on the organ, and that Dr. Elvey would be ready to begin them the next morning.

"I need not say how eagerly I embraced such a precious opportunity. I had never before played any organ but the little one of eight stops in my father's church, and had never advanced beyond hymn-tunes.

"The Doctor took great interest in me, and, besides the two lessons a week, I had two practices on the organ, and daily practices on an old piano at my lodgings.

"After the lessons were over the Doctor did me the honour to propose my taking a morning service at St. George's, but I had not the nerve for that, and gave a recital, at his suggestion, to Lord Russell and his friends instead.

"After I had finished my performance, the Doctor, at our request, extemporized a fugue. It was a splendid impromptu, and delighted me.

"I did not go again to Windsor till the winter of 1849, and, during that long interval, never had an opportunity of playing any organ, great or small.

"During the short time I was there on this second occasion, the Doctor showed me every kindness, asking me very frequently to spend an evening at his house, sometimes nearly every evening in the week. He took me also to rehearsals, and talked with me in the intervals, describing the character of the music, and pointing out special features.

"At home he played and sang to me. In one song was a shake which he did with uncommon purity.

"Again and again, but never too often, he played me Mendelssohn's 'Lieder.'

"During one of these musical evenings, I remember the two servants rushed into the room, screaming that the sky was all on fire, and the end of the world was come.

"We hastened out of doors, and found a most magnificent aurora, such as I have never since seen.

"We took out a newspaper, and found we could read it quite easily.

"On one occasion, some years later, I went with Elvey to the afternoon service at Eton. On the way he told me that he was going to have Beckwith's chant; it was not a chant he liked, but the boys had asked him for it, as they were always doing, and he couldn't refuse them.

" Most of my hymn-tunes I have sent to my old friend for his opinion, and most gratefully shall I ever remember the prompt kindness with which he attended to my request, and the suggestions which he made for their improvement. It is not long since, in writing to me, he said, ' I shall never change my style, and I advise you not to change yours.' "

CHAPTER XV.

FOR Her Majesty's birthday in 1850 the Doctor produced a cantata, which was performed before the Queen and Prince Albert at the Castle. The beautiful words for this were written by William Ball, and the programme is given in full, as doubtless it will be interesting to many.

OVERTURE.

RECITATIVE—*Mr. Lockey.*

The rolling year leads on the bounteous May,
And smiling Peace, beneath Britannia's sway,
Weaving bright gifts to grace the domes of Fame,
Now consecrates, amid the world's acclaim,
Her proudest wreath to grace Victoria's name.

AIR—*Mr. Lockey.*

Sov'reign, before whose honour'd throne,
    On this thy natal day,
Thy grateful people bow them down,
    And faithful homage pay,—
Accept, O Monarch of our hearts,
    The off'ring which we bring;
The lay our tuneful joy imparts,
    Our cheerful voices sing.

While heartfelt raptures fill the air,
   And hail the festive day,
Proclaiming thus another year,
   Of thy maternal sway:
And prayers ascend from ev'ry tongue,
   That all to thee be given
That can on earth thy reign prolong,
   And crown thy trust in heaven.

CHORUS.

The signal chime breaks on the list'ning hour,
The joyous round peals from the lofty tower;
From countless masts the ready standards fly,
And eager volleys shake the vaulted sky;
The many-sounding seas their echoes pour,
And answ'ring thunders bound from shore to shore;
"GOD SAVE THE QUEEN!" old England's myriads cry,
"GOD SAVE THE QUEEN!" her distant sons reply;
Electric fires seem round the globe to roll,
Speeding the patriot-shout from pole to pole;
And lands, erewhile of human eye unseen,
Now raise, o'er snow-clad hills or prairies green,
The all-commingling strain—
"GOD SAVE THE QUEEN!"

MADRIGAL

Through the realm, from sainted pile,
   Chapel rude, and pillar'd aisle,
Loyal supplications flow,
   And holy pray'rs their grace bestow;
Now the sacred choirs upraise
   Anthems meet of humble praise,

While the inspiring organ rolls
    Harmonious glories o'er our souls.
Whence this solemn jubilee?
QUEEN OF ALBION! 'tis for thee.
For thee our aspirations blend,
Our sceptred Dove of Peace and friend;
For thee and all—by Heav'n's decree
Thrice-blest who live endear'd to thee!

CHORUS.

Again the chime—again o'er hall and bow'r
The joyous sound peals from the lofty tow'r:
From keep and spire the far-seen banners fly,
Redoubling volleys shake the vaulted sky;
The gay parade convenes the brilliant throng,
And rich pavilions teem with dance and song.
"GOD SAVE THE QUEEN," the tuneful minstrels cry;
"GOD SAVE THE QUEEN," exulting crowds reply;
Art's mimic-stars of upward lustre spring,
And 'mid the clouds their beauteous colours fling:
Night seems to view apart the kindling scene,
In festal light moves all to life terrene,
And heart and voice rejoice—"GOD SAVE THE QUEEN."

PRAYER FOR THE ROYAL FAMILY.

SOLO—*Mrs. Alexander Newton.*

O Thou, supreme o'er earth and skies,
    Extend Thy all-sustaining hand,
And bless with all the gifts we prize
    The Sov'reign of our native land.

SOLO.

With Thy enduring aids, O Lord,
  Our royal Albert's path illume,
And life-long joys, in sweet accord,
  There wreathe with honour's fadeless plume.

CHORUS.

Great Father, guard their princely race,
  And, when the claims of earth decay,
Shed o'er the change Thy dews of grace,
  And lead them to eternal day.

FINAL CHORUS.

Thine, Britannia, evermore
  Be freedom's hallow'd ground,
Where peace and plenty love to pour
  Their choicest gifts around.
And long be thine (the crowning joy
  That greets thy matchless sway)
Through circling years the glad employ
  Of this auspicious day.
While echoing thousands load the gale,
  Waving their laurels green,
With song and shout, "VICTORIA, hail !
  All hail !—LONG LIVE THE QUEEN."

This work opens with a fine overture which introduces as a subject the National Anthem, first allotted to the wind instruments, and afterwards taken up with grand effect by the strings; then follows a recitative and beautiful tenor song, a chorus, and after this a fine madrigal, which shows the versatility of the composer's talent.   After the prayer for the Royal Family, this most interesting composition is brought to a close with a very effective and jubilant chorus.

Those who watched the faces of the royal party during the progress of the work plainly saw how delighted they were, both with the music and the way in which it was performed, and were thus a little prepared for the very kind reception the Doctor met with from Her Majesty and the Prince Consort.   At the finale they sent for him, and lavished on him their warm approbation at the treat he had, with such infinite pains and trouble, prepared for them ; neither did they forget to express the warmest pleasure at the way in which the various executants had fulfilled the parts allotted to them.

This work has frequently been given since ; the last time that the composer conducted it was at Buxton in the Jubilee year.   It was performed in Windsor the year before, and he wrote thus at the time :

" Do you remember my cantata for the Queen's birthday ? It was done at the Windsor and Eton Choral Society's last concert, and I conducted it.

We had a fair string band, and some wind instruments. I suppose this will be my last appearance
in the musical world."

In November an idea which had for some time
been evolving itself in Dr. Elvey's brain took
effect.

He had conceived the plan of having a grand
musical festival at Windsor, by way of commemoration of some of the early English Church
composers, of whom he had discovered that
several had been his predecessors at St. George's,
and it occurred to him that a public performance
of some of their works might afford much enjoyment to lovers of Cathedral music.

The idea thus conceived met with a kind and
ready response from the Dean and Canons of
Windsor. The commemoration was intended to
have been set on foot quietly, but the very extent
of the arrangements, coupled with one or two
brief announcements in the papers, rapidly spread
the news.

The following account is culled from various
newspapers which appeared at the time :

" The Royal Borough of Windsor was the
theatre on Friday last of a scene the equal of
which has not probably been witnessed in Eng-

land at any period since the Reformation. Dr. Elvey, the accomplished organist of St. George's Chapel, had conceived the felicitous idea of demonstrating to the public the majestic effect to be produced by the performance of a chronological selection from the works of our English composers of ecclesiastical music, and accordingly organized the celebration of the morning and evening Cathedral services on a large scale. As the day approached, the excitement increased, and arrangements were made for the accommodation of as many of the public as the Chapel could possibly hold. The choir was set apart for the Dean and Canons and their friends, and other persons were admitted to that rather limited space by ticket, while the nave was provided with seats, and thrown open to the public.

" As a grand performance of sacred music, got up extemporaneously and without the possibility of a rehearsal, the services of the day stand unrivalled."

At half-past ten the procession of choristers was formed in the Cloisters. In addition to the members of the Chapel choir, there were lay-vicars from the Chapel Royal, St. James's, Westminster Abbey, Canterbury, Salisbury, Worcester, and Lichfield Cathedrals; also several members of the Sacred Harmonic Society, and the organists of Gloucester, Bristol, Worcester, and Rochester.

The treble parts were strengthened by the choristers of Her Majesty's Chapel Royal and the choristers of St. Andrew's Church, Wells Street, forming altogether a choir of upwards of 100 voices.

The afternoon service was attended by Prince Albert, the Prince of Wales, and the Princess Royal.

The Rev. H. Butterfield chanted the service, and the following members of the Chapel were present: the Dean, the Hon. and Rev. Lord Wriothesley Russell, the Hon. and Rev. H. C. Cust, the Hon. and Rev. E. Moon, the Rev. W. Canning, the Rev. W. Markham, the Rev. C. Pack, and the Rev. J. Gore.

The prayers in the morning were read by the Rev. W. Markham and Lord Wriothesley Russell, and Dr. G. Elvey presided at the organ.

The solo parts were well sung by Messrs. Turner, Knowles, Marriott, Hobbs, Mudge, Bridgewater, and Whitehouse.

Then came the pealing chorus, and seldom have the fine compositions of the respective writers been rendered with such sublimity and effect.

The following is a copy of the official programme :

MORNING SERVICE.

CHANT—" Venite "—*Humphreys*, 1666.
CHANT—Ps. xxxviii., xxxix.—*Morley*, 1600.
CHANT—Ps. xl.—*From an ancient harmony. Crotch.*
TE DEUM AND BENEDICTUS—*Gibbons*, 1620.
ANTHEM—" Hosanna "—*Gibbons*, 1620.

(Gibbons was organist of the Chapel Royal.)

ANTHEM, LITANY, AND RESPONSES—*Tallis*, 1570.

(Tallis was organist of the Chapel Royal, and was the first to enrich the Cathedral service with harmony.)

ANTHEMS SUNG AFTER THE SERVICE.

"Gloria in Excelsis"—*Marbecke*, 1550.

(Marbecke was organist of St. George's Chapel, Windsor, and was the first composer of the Cathedral service. Having published his " Book of Common Prayer Noted," in 1550, he narrowly escaped martyrdom, having been convicted on a charge of favouring the Reformation, together with Anthony Pierson, Robert Testwood, and Henry Filmer. The latter was burnt below the

North Terrace of Windsor Castle ; but Marbecke obtained, through the Bishop of Winchester, the King's pardon. After this, Marbecke wrote several works against Popery.)

"Lord, for Thy tender mercies' sake"—*Richard Farrant*, 1580.

(Richard Farrant, organist of St. George's Chapel, 1580.)

"Sing we merrily unto God our strength"—*Dr. Child*, 1660.

(Dr. Child was organist of St. George's, Windsor, and was a liberal benefactor to the borough, having bequeathed a sum of money to the Corporation. He likewise paved the body of the choir at his own expense, which paving remains to this day. Dr. Child was buried in St. George's, and a stone, with his epitaph, lies close to the organ-loft door.)

"I was in the Spirit on the Lord's day"—*Dr. Blow*, 1675.

(Organist of St. Paul's Cathedral, and, upon the death of Purcell, of Westminster Abbey.)

"O, give thanks"—*Henry Purcell*, 1685.

(Organist of Westminster Abbey.)

"I have set God always before me"—*John Goldwin*, 1710.

(Organist and master of the choristers, St. George's Chapel, Windsor.)

"Cry aloud and shout "—*Dr. Croft*, 1720.

(Organist, master of the boys, and composer to the Chapel Royal.)

"God is our hope and strength "—*Dr. Greene*, 1745.

(Organist and composer to the Chapel Royal and organist of St. Paul's Cathedral.)

"O, give thanks "—*Dr. Boyce*, 1766.

(Organist and composer to the Chapel Royal.)

"In that day "—*Dr. G. J. Elvey*.

(Organist to the Queen.)

"O, praise the Lord, all ye heathen "—*Dr. G. J. Elvey*.

This anthem was written for three choirs, or twelve separate voice parts. The rehearsal of this skilful work was carried on in the nave of St. George's Chapel in order to get the proper balance of power, and to judge of the effect produced by the multiplicity of parts. The first choir opens with the subject in the plagal mode to the words of Psalm 117, "O, praise the Lord, all ye heathen;" after the development of this, the second choir sets in with another subject to the sentence, "For His merciful kindness;" an episode for the third choir is introduced to the next verse of the psalm, "And the truth of the Lord." Upon a return to the first subject, all the parts are gradually used together; then each choir separately leading on to the grand climax to the finale, "Hallelujah. Amen."

At the evening service the anthem was, "O sing unto the Lord" (Purcell).

It is impossible to do justice to this splendid performance, which was at that time quite unique. It showed Dr. Elvey's marvellous power of organization, and the extreme attention he paid to little details, so essential to the perfect success of such an undertaking.

No one can form any conception of the amount of labour required for the carrying out of such a festival. The collecting of the voices; the writing of letters in connection therewith; the selecting of the music, which, in many cases, had to be copied; the rehearsal of each choir separately; and the amount of experience required to hold all these atoms together, necessitates an amount of skill which at that day was seldom to be met with.

"The pealing tones of the magnificent organ, played with the masterly ability of Dr. Elvey, and responded to by a choir at once so numerous and so correct, chiming in with its multitude of voices, with all the precision of a perfect and well-regulated machine, was productive of an effect which could only be appreciated by those present, and which is unsusceptible of description."

The best judges of music pronounced the performance perfect, and the Dean and Canons expressed their great delight, and thanked Dr. Elvey for the immense trouble he had taken. At the close of the afternoon service Prince Albert asked for a repetition of his anthem, "In that day," and it was given with, if possible, increased effect.

The service ended, the whole of the choir proceeded to the Castle, and beneath the dining-room windows serenaded the Queen and the Royal Family with the National Anthem.

They most graciously acknowledged this exhibition of devotion and loyalty by appearing at the windows and bowing. Three cheers were then given for Her Majesty; and thus ended a festival long to be remembered in Windsor—ever afterwards designated as the "Festival of the Ancients."

CHAPTER XVI.

IN the Great International Exhibition of 1851 three magnificent organs were erected, and upon one of these Dr. Elvey was requested to perform on the opening day.

The St. George's choir were also engaged to take part. The arrival of the party at Paddington was most disastrous. A steady downpour of rain had churned the London mud into a black paste. No vehicle was to be had, and the choir had to make their way, as best they could, from the railway station to Hyde Park under dripping umbrellas.

According to previous arrangement, Dr. Elvey appeared at the Exhibition arrayed in his robes, and intense was his amusement at the effect produced on the crowd, and even on the stolid policemen by his gorgeous apparel. With cries of " Make way, make way," he was ushered into the building, and exploding with merriment, quickly made his way to the organ.

Amongst other pieces he played Handel's "Hallelujah Chorus" as a duet with Dr. Wilde.

The organization of the choirs was anything but perfect. They were huddled together in the gallery without knowing quite who was to be the conductor, or where the music was to come from. Sir George Smart, upon a given signal, began to conduct with a baton having a large gold crown on the top, but the voices were not properly distributed, and, some having parts and some not, the effect was far from satisfactory.

During this exhibition the Cologne Choir were in England; they came to Windsor and sang some German Lieder in the nave of St. George's, under the direction of Herr Lindpaintner, Dr. Elvey interspersing the vocal pieces with selections on the organ. Their singing was magnificent, and the crescendos and diminuendos came in waves of sound up the nave from the west end with remarkable effect, which made an impression never to be forgotten upon those who had the privilege of hearing it.

Doubtless it was the remembrance of this musical treat which induced him to pay a brief visit to Cologne a few years after.

Later in the year, the first start was made with

what is now so widely known as " The Choir Benevolent Fund."   The design of this fund was to secure a provision for aged and invalid members, to guarantee a fixed sum payable at the decease of members to their widows and children, and also to afford temporary assistance in time of need or affliction.

These objects were to be accomplished by an annual contribution from the organists and lay-clerks connected with the cathedral and collegiate choirs, and by an appeal to the sympathy and kindness of all those interested in choral worship and the perpetuation of the works of great com-posers of English church music. Subsequently, the committee were enabled to extend their original work, and the widows of former members of the society received an additional sum of £10 10s.

The fund was established under the patronage of H.M. the Queen and a large number of digni-taries of the Church.

The first committee meeting was held in Dr. Elvey's drawing-room in the Cloisters, and he was ever after a warm supporter of the fund.

He and his brother Stephen both took im-mense interest in its development and extension, and worked hard for it in many ways.

The report of the Society for 1853 speaks thus of the assistance rendered by them :

"The unwearied exertions of Dr. G. J. Elvey, organist of Windsor, and of Dr. Elvey, organist of New College, Oxford, deserve high commendation, both of these gentlemen having devoted much valuable time to the service of the Society, in making the requisite preliminary arrangements."

The fund was partly indebted for its support to the proceeds of festivals which were held in various parts of the country.

Many of these, on a large scale, took place in St. George's Chapel; among them the first ever held in aid of the fund, in 1853.

Later on, Dr. Elvey became a member of the committee of management, and subsequent festivals were held in the Chapel in 1857, 1866, and 1876. Although somewhat anticipating the course of events, it may be mentioned here that the second of these festivals (1866) was the most successful (from a financial point of view, at least), probably owing to the fact that it took place the day after the wedding of H.R.H. Princess Christian, for which a great many strangers had come into the neighbourhood.

Early in the morning the people began to assemble, and by about eleven o'clock the beautiful building was full. The congregation included many of the Queen's guests who were staying at the Castle. The choir was, as usual, strengthened by gentlemen and choristers from Westminster Abbey, St. Paul's Cathedral, and the Chapel Royal, St. James's. Nearly a hundred voices assisted in rendering the music with a degree of perfection that only Cathedral choristers and lay-clerks can attain.

After the service a succession of anthems was given, concluding with " Sing unto God," composed by Dr. Elvey in honour of the marriage of the Prince of Wales.

This was particularly appropriate to the occasion, in view of the royal wedding which had taken place on the previous day.

The anthem was ushered in with a symphony, in which were combined the merry peal of bells, the triumphant blast of trumpets, and other joyous sounds.

The collection at this service, after paying all expenses, added £108 to the funds of the society.

In the evening, those who had taken part in the morning's service assisted at a concert which was given (also in aid of the fund) in St. Mark's Schools.

A number of glees and madrigals, etc., were performed.

The double work entailed by these two performances was very fatiguing for Dr. Elvey, but the immense interest he always took in his work, and his unwearied enthusiasm, carried him steadily over obstacles which would have repelled and crushed many a less vigorous and persevering character.

Gradually a shadow crept over his home, for Mrs. Elvey, who for some time had been frail and weakly, began to develop signs of depression and disease.

Week after week passed away, and the light of the home grew fainter and fainter. Month followed month; doctors were summoned for consultation. Old medical friends hied from London, only to confirm the sad news that the delicate woman had become a bedridden invalid. A terrible blow was this, indeed, to her devoted husband, who seemed stunned and incapable of action. Frequently young Verrinder played the service at the Chapel, whilst Dr. Elvey sat sobbing by his side.

The former proved to him at this time a most kind and able assistant, training the choir, carrying on his correspondence, and in every way seeking to lighten his burden of care and sorrow.

In July the cloud which had been overhanging so long burst upon him, and his devotedly loved and truly saintly wife passed to her eternal rest.

Deeply did her husband and child mourn her loss; but, terrible as was the blow, and broken-hearted though he was, he felt that he must now rouse himself and again take up the threads of his work, with which no personal feelings were long allowed to interfere. Thus, not many months after, we again find him preparing an anthem for the Gloucester Festival, the words of which he took from the 97th Psalm.

Whilst composing this anthem his sister-in-law was busy working at some embroidery on a frame, and as the silk passed through the tightly-stretched canvas it made a noise resembling thunder. He was at this time writing the chorus, "Clouds and Darkness," and begged her to work as fast and as long as she could, that the sound of her needle might give him the needful inspiration.

This anthem, as usual, he scored for an orchestra.

It was a splendid work, and was received with great approbation.

A gentleman thus wrote at the time:

"By request Dr. Elvey has composed an anthem for the Gloucester Festival. He has adapted passages from the 97th Psalm as part of his text, and the words of the Psalmist have inspired him with the happiest thoughts that have yet helped him to rank honourably among our most meritorious composers for the Church.

" This anthem is in D major, and it opens with a spirited chorus, ' The Lord is King,' and terminates with a clever fugato, ' For His mercy endureth for ever.'

" It abounds in beautiful passages, and the choruses are very grand and massive. The principal singers, orchestra, and chorus appear to vie with each other in giving effect to it. The chorus, 'Clouds and Darkness,' is exceedingly effective, and the double chorus, 'At His sight the mountains are shaken,' is dramatic in expression, the music being made to convey the spirit of the words.

" The concluding chorus is a clever specimen of writing, and displays Dr. Elvey's ability as a composer.

" This anthem will bear frequent repetition at festivals, being a work of more than ordinary merit."

Dr. Elvey, as usual, took part of his choir to this festival, and himself conducted his anthem.

Another work that occupied a great deal of his time during these solitary years was arranging the " Messiah " and " Judas Maccabæus " for piano or organ, with vocal score, for Surman, The plates of this splendid edition of the noble Saxon's works were unfortunately bought, at Surman's death, by another music publisher, and, it is believed, were destroyed, greatly to the regret of those who know what a perfect edition this was.

All the choruses, etc., bore the metronome marks made by Dr. Elvey with extreme care, in order to preserve the traditional time as he had received it, in direct succession from the composer.

The autumn of the year 1852 is memorable in Windsor for the worst flood of the century.

Eton was quite under water, the floods reaching the bottom of the Hundred Steps ; and as this occurred just at the time of the death of England's hero, the Duke of Wellington, it was always called the " Wellington Flood."

K

The "Iron" Duke's funeral was the next important event in which the Doctor took part.

At six o'clock on the eventful morning (November 18th), he made his way with his choir to St. Paul's Cathedral, there to join in the solemn service, England's last tribute of respect to the hero of Waterloo. It was a grand, solemn, and impressive sight.

Speaking of the Duke, one is reminded of an amusing story that Dr. Elvey used to tell.

Upon one occasion, entering one of the Royal Chapels with his spurs on, the chorister boys spied him, and after service, according to an ancient custom, surrounded him and demanded "spur-money."

To this he replied, "Say your gamut," and nothing would he give them until this was done.

Asking for spur-money was an old custom at Canterbury when Sir George was a boy, and he used to relate with amusement how startled an old farmer would often be when, having wandered into the Cathedral on market-day, the choristers, ever on the watch, pounced on him for this fine.

This old custom he re-introduced at St. George's, and, greatly to the surprise of some unwary gentlemen who rode into Windsor to attend the service, and clinked, all unheeding, into the Chapel with their spurs, they were caught, as soon as service was over, and not permitted to quit the building until some of their superfluous cash was transferred to the pockets of the eager boys.

CHAPTER XVII.

IN 1853 the Chapel organ was again rebuilt and enlarged by Messrs. Gray and Davison, under Dr. Elvey's superintendence.

New reeds were added, and considerable additions and alterations made to the stops.

The hautboy in the swell organ was replaced by an oboe, and a new double-trumpet, cornopean, and clarion were added.

The great organ was fitted with a new posaune and clarion.

In the choir organ the bassoon was replaced by a piccolo, and the clarionet by a corno di basseto.

To the pedal organ were added principal and posaune.

The copulæ were augmented by swell to choir, and choir sub-octave to great.

New action and soundboards were added, and a pneumatic draw-stop with noiseless action ; also additional thickness to the swell-box, and a new set of Venetian swell-shutters opening into the nave.

Of these, Dr. Verrinder says that the wonderful effect produced of the sound being thrown into the nave by their means was kept a profound secret, so that it might not be imitated.

It is believed that this effect was quite unique, and did not exist in any other Cathedral church.

During the progress of the work, H.R.H. the Prince Consort took great interest in it, and used to come down to the Chapel accompanied by his two elder sons, and examine the pipes as they were lying about the nave in heaps, ready to be placed in the new sounding-boards.

The Prince examined each set of pipes very carefully, and tried some of the smaller ones by blowing into them with his mouth, and an eye-witness relates how amusing it was to see the two young Princes endeavouring to follow the paternal example.

When the bellows were removed for repair, amongst the rubbish was found a set of books of oblong shape that had been hidden during the Commonwealth. They contained services and anthems in single parts, printed in lozenge-shaped notes, without bars, and in four lines. They were chiefly written by the early fathers of Cathedral music, Tomkins, Tallis, and Byrde.

Some of these were transcribed into score by the Doctor and his pupils, and the missing parts were supplied by his master hand. One or more of these services was afterwards published by the well-known antiquarian, Dr. Rimbault.

When the work of restoration was finished, the critics set about finding fault. The Dean said the choir reed grated upon and offended his ears, and some others complained that the pedal reed was too loud. Many were the journeys from London to Windsor, and *vice versâ*, between Messrs. Gray and Davison's factory and the Chapel organ, undertaken by Dr. Elvey, to satisfy himself, and to meet the objections of those in authority, and others who had no claim or knowledge to offer an opinion.

But constant dropping will wear away a stone, and these reiterated remarks so worked upon his sensitive disposition that one morning Dr. Elvey went quietly up to the organ-loft, took the clarionet out of its place in the choir-organ, put the pipes in a salmon-basket, and packed off one of the boys by train, fish-basket and all, to Messrs. Gray and Davison's factory in the Euston Road.

The firm, being desirous of doing all that could be done to make amends, determined on sending to Windsor one of their best and most skilful finishers.

The choice fell upon Mr. Mitchell, brother-in-law to Mr. Davison.

This gentleman, on a certain Saturday, went down quietly to the royal precincts to judge of the effect of the various stops during the Sunday services, and to be ready to commence operations early on Monday morning.

Mr. Mitchell and his assistants reached the Chapel at 7 a.m. and had scarcely begun to work when, at 7.15, Dr. Elvey, clad in his dressing-gown, and very little else, rushed from his house to the sacred edifice, and shouted with all his might and main, as soon as he reached the Chapel door : "Mr. Mitchell, Mr. Mitchell, you'll wake the Dean !"

Onward came the sound, and up the organ-loft stairs like a cat came Dr. Elvey. When the tumult had subsided, and he arrived near the keyboards, considerably winded, Mr. Mitchell replied :

" I have come down on purpose to do what you wish with the trombone. You tell me I shall wake the Dean ; you say at nine o'clock he will be at his breakfast, and must not be disturbed—further, that at 10.30 the service begins. When can I do the trombone ? "

The hour was fixed for after morning prayers at 11.30.

Meanwhile, having taken breakfast, Mr. Mitchell repaired to the North Terrace to enjoy the air and view ; and, filling his pipe, began to puff vigorously, dreaming, amid the clouds of smoke, that his troubles were ended. Vain hope ! A monstrous spectre in the shape of a grenadier stood over him, with musket lowered and bayonet fixed, ready to charge. In loud accents and in threatening attitude he thus delivered himself :

" I have been calling to ye ever so long, telling ye not to smoke there. If ye don't stop, I'll very soon put your pipe out for ye ! "

" Why may I not smoke here ? "

" It ain't allowed ! Don't ye see the notice board, or can't ye read ? "

Disconcerted, Mitchell took the next train back to London, and reported to his chief that he had been to Windsor to cure the trombone. He had not been allowed to work at seven because he would wake the Dean ; at nine that important dignitary could not be disturbed at his breakfast.

At 10.30 the service would occupy the rest of the morning. At 4.30 p.m. was another service. He had better send a man whose time was not so valuable; but, before he started, he should like to give him a few words of counsel by way of warning; for he was not permitted to walk or smoke on the Terrace, and nearly lost his life in the attempt. Never more would he set foot in the place, as long as he lived, if he could help it.

When questioned on the subject some years later Mitchell declared he still kept to his determination.

During the cholera visitation of the autumn of 1853 many cases occurred in Windsor, chiefly in the low-lying and badly-built houses by the riverside. The terrible disease was a source of great apprehension to the Doctor, who used to see from his windows the carts calling at the houses for the dead bodies.

Years afterwards he used to relate how, on going across to Chapel in the morning, the thought would haunt him that perhaps he might not live to play the evening service.

This nervous anxiety at length affecting his health, he went to Oxford, where he stayed with his brother Stephen, hoping by this means to distract his thoughts.

The spectre of cholera, however, continually haunted him. He had not been at Oxford long when a boating party was organized in his honour.

Shortly after a start had been made, one of the party entered into conversation with Dr. Elvey, commencing with some remarks about the prevailing malady, and adding the gruesome information that there were a good many cases in Oxford, especially by the river-side !

About this time, Mr. John Nichols, editor of the " Gentleman's Magazine," took one of the Canons' houses in the Cloisters, and through him and Mrs. Nichols, Dr. Elvey was introduced to his second wife, whom he married in 1854.

They had five children, four of whom are now living.

Dr. Elvey's much-loved brother, Dr. Stephen Elvey, was, during this period, very busy with the preparation of his Psalter—a work that occupied him for seven years. Every verse was carefully studied, and in all cases of doubt the most learned men in Oxford were consulted, and the original Hebrew referred to. It was Elvey who introduced the imaginary bar, and every Psalter that has since appeared is simply a reproduction of his, with a few alterations. Rarely, if ever, can they be styled improvements.

Dr. Stephen was a man, not only of splendid musical attainments, but a devout and earnest Christian, and he devoted all his splendid powers to this work.

His pointing of the Psalms is quite a commentary on the words, and where the latter is used, as it is, even in many small agricultural villages, the rough chanting of the Psalms by country lads is rendered intelligible.

One summer during this period Dr. Stephen spent his vacation of seven weeks at Windsor, and so entranced was he with his work, that the cessation from more active duties only meant increased time spent on this.

His pockets were filled with bits of paper, with verses from the Psalms written upon them, in different forms and with different readings, and these he used to discuss with anyone likely to be interested in the subject.

Dr. Verrinder, who was then at Windsor, says : " I remember his pulling up suddenly in one of the principal streets of the town, and, to the astonishment of passers-by, asking me in anything but a whisper :

"'What is a manpeace?'

"'I don't know.'

"'Neither do I ; but when chanted the error of putting the accent on *man* instead of *peace* is almost universal, and is an instance of the nonsense made of passages in Scripture through careless reading and indifferent punctuation.'   The verse runs thus: 'Keep innocency, and take heed unto the thing that is right, for that shall bring a man peace at the last.'

"Said he, 'I requested my friend Dr. Morris, a Fellow of New College, Oxford, to sing that passage to me, and he fell into the trap at once, but when he read the verse, he of course gave the correct rendering.'

"Another question he asked me was, 'Have you studied the characters in Pickwick?'

"I said I had never had the chance of seeing the works of Dickens, but I possessed those of Scott.

"'Oh! how I wish I could say that!' he replied. 'The pleasure of reading Pickwick the first time I can scarcely realize. I have gone through the book sixteen times, and can find something fresh to laugh at every time!'"

"On Sundays, during his stay at the Cloisters,

the two brothers Elvey played duets as organ voluntaries. They usually selected something by Handel or Crotch, but I think only because the compositions were best adapted for the purpose by reason of the massiveness of their construction.

" I would here take the opportunity of correcting a mistake which seems to have become rather widespread and far-reaching, viz., that the Elveys had no sympathy with modern composers, and were out of touch with everything later than Handel ! Nothing could be further from the truth.

" Haydn, Mozart, Beethoven, Spohr, Mendelssohn, and Bennett were in daily use, and their slow movements turned into voluntaries for the organ.

" I have many times re-arranged Dr. Elvey's music cupboard, where his teaching stock was kept, and can affirm most positively that, besides the ordinary fashionable drawing-room pieces of the day, he had, for those pupils with higher views and nobler aspirations, more of Beethoven, Mozart, and Mendelssohn than of all the rest put together."

(These remarks of Dr. Verrinder's can be fully confirmed by his pupils, who know his ardent admiration for Beethoven, in whose sonatas he revelled ; and none who have heard him can readily forget his exquisite rendering of these works.

Besides these, he delighted in Haydn, Weber, Mendelssohn, and Mozart; and of later, and perhaps lighter composers, he enjoyed and admired Schumann, Chopin, Heller, and Rossini; so that to say he was simply a Handelian, and little or nothing else, is as absurd as it is incorrect.[1]

But he did not admire that modern music, which, forsaking all rules, is for ever striving after an effect to which it never attains.)

" That the brothers Elvey were unsparing in their condemnation of any ·but the recognized method of interpreting Handel's oratorios, I grant,

---

[1] The following letter, written by Dr. Arnold of Winchester, after Sir George's death, is inserted as an illustration of this :

" I do not consider your late husband was only a Handelian; he was a continuation of the school of English musicians who have a *style of their own*, based upon the Church and madrigal writers. Where is there any resemblance in ' Wherewithal ' or ' In that Day ' to Handel? .

" His style was purely English, and his counterpoint of a very high order. This the middle chorus of ' In that Day ' will amply prove to any unprejudiced observer.

" I deeply regret his departure, for, setting aside his musical ability, as a man he was just and honest, and could be trusted."

and in this they were not singular, for Mendelssohn was equally strong on the point. Dr. Stephen Elvey once went to Exeter Hall to hear 'Israel in Egypt' given by the Sacred Harmonic Society, and when they reached the 'Hailstone Chorus' he could not contain himself any longer. He had hitherto confined himself to quiet grunts of disapproval, but now he launched out into—' You may call those hailstones, if you like; but *I* call them peas!'

"As the remembrance of him floats before me, I recall with pleasure a lovely Mendelssohnian duet of his, part of a selection from an oratorio by him once performed by the Windsor and Eton Choral Society."

His brother George fully shared his objections to any interference with Handel's works.

Once, when conducting a rehearsal of the "Messiah," one of the lady principals finished her solo with an elaborate cadenza. Sir George waited until the end, and then said, "What's *that?* Don't you think that if Handel had wanted that he would have written it?" "Oh! we always do it in London," replied the lady. "Never mind," he answered, "*here* Handel shall have it in *his* way, so please sing it as it is written."

Upon the death of Dr. Walmisley, Professor of Music to the University of Cambridge, Dr. Elvey sent in his name as 'a candidate for the post, but he did not succeed in obtaining it, although he was very ably supported.

This, however, never disturbed his pleasant intercourse with Sir Sterndale Bennett (his successful rival), for whom he ever entertained a warm affection, and of whose abilities he thought most highly.

It may be interesting to record one of many testimonials that Dr. Elvey received at this time, bearing witness to his great abilities, which, from his modest and retiring disposition, never received due recognition.

" I wish to give the strongest testimony I can to the merit of Dr. George J. Elvey, who is, I understand, a candidate for the office of Professor of Music in the University of Cambridge. It would be difficult, in my opinion, to find a man better qualified than he is in every way for this most important post, and I should rejoice indeed if his claims be recognized as they deserve, and I have no hesitation in saying that, whether as a contrapuntist, a skilful and correct organist, or a most conscientious and high-principled man, Dr. Elvey will yield to few, if any.

(Signed) " FREDERICK A. GORE OUSELEY,
M.A., Bart., Precentor of Hereford, Professor of Music in the University of Oxford."

Similar testimonials were received from Sir John Goss, organist of St. Paul's Cathedral, Edward Taylor, Gresham Professor of Music, and from many others.

CHAPTER XVIII.

DURING these years Dr. Elvey had a large circle of private pupils, by all of whom he was regarded with an immense amount of esteem and respect.

He was a splendid teacher, sparing no pains and leaving no stone unturned to secure the end he wished to attain ; and his methods exerted an almost magic influence in inspiring his pupils with something of the enthusiasm and love for work which so characterized the master.

He would nearly always accompany his pupils on the violin, while sometimes the double-bass, or the drums, would be pressed into the service to give effect to the lesson he was trying to impart.

Mention has been made of the lessons he gave H.R.H. the Duke of Cambridge and Prince Edward of Saxe-Weimar, and, later on, H.R.H. the Prince Consort and T.R.H. the Princesses Christian and Beatrice.

Among his articled pupils are names which have

made their mark on the music of the day.   Of
these may be mentioned :

C. G. Verrinder, Mus. Doc., organist of St.
Mary's, West Kensington.

E. H. Thorne, Mus. Bac., organist of St. Anne's,
Soho.

Haydn Keeton, Mus. Doc., organist of Peter-
borough Cathedral.

C. Huntley, Mus. Doc., organist, Newcastle-on-
Tyne.

J. S. Liddle, Mus. Bac., organist of Newbury.

Chas. Hancock, Mus. Bac., organist of St.
Martin's, Leicester.

The list of his private pupils is a very long one.
It included the Duchess of Malakoff, the Hon.
Victoria Grosvenor, the Hon. E. M. Russell, Miss
Phipps, Miss Van de Weyer, the Misses Anson,
Miss Biddulph, the Misses Vansittart; also the
Duke of Newcastle, Lord Edward Clinton, Sir
Stevenson Blackwood, Mr. R. H. M. Bosanquet,
Fellow of St. John's College, Oxford, Mr. Edward
Hamilton.   Professor Hubert Parry, Mus. Doc.,
the eminent musician and author, who has since
become so famous, owes his early education in
music to Sir George Elvey.   When a boy at Eton
he was constantly in the organ-loft on Sundays

and his early impressions have left their mark upon his recent works.

The exercise for Dr. Hubert Parry's Mus. Bac. degree and other works were examined and corrected by his old master.

When Dr. Bridge, organist of Westminster Abbey and Gresham Professor, was organist of Holy Trinity, Windsor, he became a pupil of Dr. Elvey's, whose style has not been without its effect on his music, more especially in his larger compositions, and those written for his Mus. Bac. and Mus. Doc. degrees.

" In my Eton days, from 1840 to 1849," writes Mr. A. D. Coleridge, " St. George's Chapel was a never-failing attraction to any boy with musical instincts. I thought at that time, and I believe now, that no choral body in England retained, year after year, so uniform a level of excellence as that over which Sir George presided.

" He had difficulties to contend with from which no organist is exempt. For the first few years of his office his merits had been acknowledged by William IV. and his Queen, who constantly attended the Chapel services ; the young organist basked in the sunshine of royal approbation.

" The melodious and well-known anthem,

'Wherewithal shall a young man cleanse his way,' was written especially for the confirmation of the Duke, then Prince George of Cambridge. A royal request that Elvey would write music for the occasion was obviously a compliment, and a cheering recognition of services already felt and valued in high quarters.

" I spoke of the difficulties from which no organist in those days was exempt ; for superannuated tenors and basses, whose vested privileges were not to be interfered with, existed at St. George's Chapel as well as elsewhere.

" But the vocal imperfections of these veterans were so skilfully veiled and kept in the background, that, during the many years of my attendance, I never heard a chant, service, or anthem which were perceptibly marred by coarse or inferior singing.

" The boys were invariably in a high state of training and discipline. Mr. French, then schoolmaster, was a cultivated man, who heartily co-operated with the young organist, zealous beyond his fellows, and whose pride in his choir was unabated from the first years of his appointment to the last day when he resigned his post.

*   *   *   *   *

" J. C. Patteson, the Martyr-Bishop of Melanesia, was as fond of St. George's Chapel as I was.

" On Sunday afternoons, in the summer half, when the Chapel was crowded, the upper stalls filled by grandees, and the lower seats tenanted by the 'poor Knights of Windsor,' it was our constant privilege to be allowed seats in the organ-loft.

" It was a treat to watch, as well as to listen to Sir George's masterly accompaniment, especially in the Handelian anthems, which I maintain were given with greater finish and brilliancy at St. George's Chapel than in any other place of worship in England.

" The Chandos and Coronation anthems, the Funeral anthem written in honour of Queen Caroline, once heard in St. George's Chapel when Elvey and his choir were at their best, can never be forgotten by those who heard them.

" Bishop Thirlwall was one of Elvey's great admirers, and, at a later date, Canon Pearson.

*　　*　　*　　*　　*

" Elvey's loyalty and devotion to his duties at St. George's Chapel made a lasting impression on his many friends at Windsor and Eton.

"We old Etonians date our love of sacred music from the time when we first heard it interpreted by him."

*   *   *   *   *

The Eton boys were frequent visitors to Dr. Elvey's organ-loft; indeed, they used to flock round him to such an extent that he used to say they did not even leave him elbow-room to play.

To many of them he gave lessons ; in fact, to quote from a well-known musical authority :

"Most of the nobility who were educated at Eton, and many eminent statesmen of this and past times, were instructed by Sir George Elvey."

From this connection with Eton he learnt much of what went on in the College in the old days, and he used to tell some amusing tales concerning Dr. Keate, the then Head Master.

At that time, from want of efficient control and systematic management, the College was at a very low ebb, and the houses were in many cases almost empty.

This was rather a sore subject with the teaching fraternity, and one day, during some discussion on the subject, one master announced, with no attempt to conceal the pride he felt at his ability to deliver so startling a proclamation, " I have ten boys returning ! "

But the fall of his pride was not far distant. When school reopened only *one* pupil appeared.

The following Sunday old Dr. Keate preached a sermon on the ten lepers, and during his discourse he made a pause, and, looking over at the master, who occupied a front seat, he repeated, very emphatically, fixing the unfortunate man with his eagle eye, " But where are the nine ? " This he did two or three times, to the no small discomfort of the boastful tutor.

Here is another funny tale of Eton concerning the boys. They had acquired a habit, which seemed to afford them unlimited pleasure, of pulling Dr. Keate's bell as often as the vigilance of their superiors admitted. Several times the irate pedagogue ran out to catch them, and the boys determining to take advantage of this, one evening placed a bag of soot on the doorstep, and rang the bell as before.

Dr. Keate rushed out, and, embracing the soft, black mass, exclaimed, in triumphant accents, " Ah ! I've caught you at last ! "

Dr. Elvey was always very fond of boys, and exercised quite a fatherly care over his pupils and choristers. He always said that he had been a chorister himself, and he sympathized greatly with boys, as he knew what they frequently had to put up with; and, although a firm disciplinarian, and particular that their work should be well done, he was yet an extremely kind friend, and, when they left, was always ready to lend a helping hand to advance their future prospects.

Mr. George Pearson, organist of Redhill, in writing says:

"As a master he was very strict with us as boys, never allowing a mistake in the music, or any misbehaviour to pass unpunished. I remember on one occasion—it was on the 4th of June, the great aquatic festival at Eton. I suppose our heads were full of what was to take place in the evening, and something went wrong in the service. What it was I do not now remember, but I *do* remember most vividly his, to us, terrible countenance as we came out of the choir. We knew what it meant; he would do his duty, if we did not; with the result that, I fear, we took the first part of our pleasure rather sadly.

" But, on the other hand, when we did well, many a sixpence found its way out of his pocket into ours, and in many ways he would try and interest us, and so help to lessen the drudgery of the usual routine. He made us fear him, but we also loved him very dearly. During the time I was in the choir we made him a present of a ring, and great was our anxiety to know if it would be accepted. When he came up the aisle, before service, with the ring on his finger, our delight knew no bounds. I feel sure that if any boy from another choir should venture to suggest that there was a kinder man or a more able musician living, we were, one and all, ready to back our sentiments in a manner peculiar, but most convincing, amongst boys.

"When I came to be under him as a pupil, it was the same principle in his actions—thoroughness and strictness, combined with kindness and encouragement.

"When his pupils had finished their course of instruction, and were started in life, a letter was sent to, and received from him, once during the week. If, from any cause, it was delayed, the question in his next was always, ' How are you getting on ? Is everything going right ? '

" For my own part, at this period of my life, I can speak of him with peculiar affection. I was living with an uncle, who just at this time died;

consequently I was being launched upon the world almost like a ship without a rudder. The Doctor took me by the hand, and from that time to the end he has been to me as a father."

*   *   *   *   *

Dr. Elvey was ever ready to lend a helping hand to anybody in need. On several occasions he took articled pupils without the slightest re-muneration, and gave them the excellent musical education which enables them now to hold first-rate posts. To more than one Elvey not only gave an education, but he and Mrs. Elvey col-lected the funds to maintain them during the time of training.

The sympathy he felt for the boys evinced itself in ways not always to be expected.

For instance, some thirty years ago it was not an uncommon thing for him to have to chastise one or other of his choristers for carelessness and faults during Divine service, but the caning never troubled a boy much ; for he knew that, whilst the ordeal itself was but slight, he was pretty sure to be taken into Dr. Elvey's dining-room afterwards to have a glass of wine. For the master appeared to have a dread lest his pupil should resent his punishment.

In this connection a tradition may be mentioned that was prevalent amongst his boys, although its accuracy cannot be vouched for. It was to the effect that, having occasion to administer corporal punishment to a boy one winter's evening in the room of his house used for the boys' practice, the solitary light being from a candle held by one of his articled pupils, the boy blew this out, upon which Dr. Elvey was so alarmed that he rushed from the room.

A letter from an "old boy" speaks of Dr. Elvey's extreme kindness to him during the years he was in the choir, and dwells especially on the care taken of himself and his fellow-choristers when they travelled with the Doctor to sing at Exeter Hall, or to Bristol, where they annually took part in the concerts of the Madrigal Society.

It also relates how, when he left the choir, Dr. Elvey obtained a good appointment for him through a friend, and also kept up a correspondence with him for many years.

Such was the affection and respect he entertained for his old master, that he came from Torquay to attend the funeral.

Another, who was also a chorister at St. George's, writes as follows :

" The Doctor's kindliness of heart towards those who had been under him as choristers was illustrated by what he did on my behalf as recently as 1889. For many years he had been a member of the committee for the society known as the 'Choir Benevolent Fund,' but for some little time, owing to his advanced age, he had not attended the meetings. At the end of 1888 the secretary, one of the few paid officers of the society, announced his intention of resigning, and I was invited by some of the members to become a candidate for the post.

" There were others, however, who nominated a rival, and the election was to take place at the general meeting of the members on February 7th, 1889. It was nearly twenty-three years since I left St. George's, and Sir George Elvey was just seventy-three years old, but he nevertheless came to London on a cold winter's day to address the members on my behalf, and the voting resulted in my election.

" During the latter part of my time at Windsor, I was the fastest runner in the school, and was rather noted for the long strides I took.

" For about a quarter of an hour between dinner and afternoon school, we played at various games on fine days in the Castle yard, and sometimes Dr. Elvey would stand out there watching us, and talking with Mr. Bransom, our master. On one occasion, when he saw me running, he called out—quoting from the words of Handel's ‘Acis and Galatea’—‘See! what ample strides he takes,’ and the boys, making a parody, continued the quotation with, ‘The Round Tower nods, the Castle shakes.’"

Another pupil writes: "I greatly esteemed him, and shall ever feel deeply indebted to him for all his kindness to me. He was ever genial and kind, and spared no pains or trouble in helping us forward. I shall never forget his harmony lessons, which were often given when out walking with me, and musical illustrations were frequently written on a white gate—no paper being at hand.

"I think the gates about Windsor Forest were studded with these little illustrations.

"It was novel, and certainly left its impression on our minds."

CHAPTER XIX.

IT was a rule of Dr. Elvey's that the reeds of the organ should be tuned by his pupils every Saturday, and for this purpose a box of tools was kept in the organ-loft.

He was always very nervous of anything happening to the organ on these occasions, and the following catechism would generally take place :

" Have you put the organ in good order, ready for to-morrow ?

" Did you use the shade ?

" I hope you have not left any of the swell-shutters out, or the tuning-flaps down!

" Did Davenport see that all was right afterwards, and that you did not set the organ on fire ?

" I almost fancy I can see a light through the windows now."

Having had his fears calmed, and been assured that all had been left perfectly safe, and the books turned at the proper places ready for his use on the morrow, he would take his dinner in comfort, and then smoke the cheroot of peace. Yet, in the cool of evening, he frequently took the keys, and made his way to the Chapel to take a last fond look into the cold and dark building, in order to satisfy himself that all was right.

On Sunday, if a pedal note stuck down, on to the bellows one of the pupils had to go, in spite of best clothes, on his back, or on hands and knees, over dust and candle-grease—the accumulation of ages—to splice a broken tracker, or pull down a pallet which had got fixed inside the wind-chest.

*   *   *   *   *

The following rather amusing account is given by Dr. Verrinder :

" At a very early period of life Dr. Elvey acquired the habit of taking snuff, and when deep in thought would dispose of pinch after pinch.

" Mrs. Elvey and many friends did their best to break him of this, but to no purpose. At last, they extracted from him promises, first, that he would restrict himself to a small quantity per diem, and secondly, that he would not carry a snuff-box.

" This was rather a trial to him, and oftentimes he would say to Thorne or myself during chapel-time, 'I am dying for a pinch of snuff; I wish you would run down to Snook's, the tobacconist in Thames Street, and get me a half-ounce of brown rappee!'

"After taking his fill he would quietly pocket snuff, paper, and all, and beam with contentment as long as it lasted. Then one of the boys had to make another pilgrimage to Snook's, always in mortal dread that Mrs. Elvey should look from the window and find him out!"

Many people, noticing Dr. Elvey's habit of having a twist of paper to hold his snuff, and thinking that they were anticipating his wishes, kindly gave him presents of various more or less handsome snuff-boxes.

Among these was a splendid silver box from the Provost and Fellows of Eton College, for permitting his pupil, now Dr. Verrinder, to occupy their organist's place for three months.

On its arrival he called Verrinder into the drawing-room, and after showing him the beautifully-engraved box, he remarked, with a merry twinkle in his eye, as he replaced it in its case, "I think next time they must give *you* a snuff-box!"

Although, in addition to this, he possessed

several other silver boxes, he did not care to use them, as he always made endeavours to check the habit of snuff-taking, and for this reason would not permit himself to carry a box in his pocket. Having consideration, however, for the feelings of others, he did not like to appear ungrateful, and would always send home for one of the boxes when the donor was expected to visit the organ-loft. The snuff was emptied into it, for he would say, "It won't do for him to see me using the paper!"

Yet, no sooner had the giver departed, than the snuff was duly returned to the paper, and the box to its companions.

He would never allow himself to procure more than half an ounce at a time. The boys' journeys to the shop being so frequent, they found it advisable to purchase two separate packets, and so keep one in stock until it was required.

He was averse to taking the snuff home with him, and usually kept it in the organ-loft, apparently hoping to get through each evening without its assistance. He, however, could seldom accomplish this, and Mr. Hancock, one of his pupils, says, "He usually asked me during the evening to fetch his packet. This I always did in the dark, for he would on no account run the risk of having a match struck in the Chapel. Sometimes he would accompany me as far as the outer door of the building, and keep guard there whilst I went upstairs. On one or two occasions only did he himself venture so far as the organ-loft; he would then leave me on guard below. Once I moved from my post, and when he descended and dimly saw a figure standing in the aisle awaiting him, he fairly shouted with fright!" Thus will snuff and a guilty conscience make cowards of us all.

After Sir George left Windsor he gave up the habit of taking snuff, and in his peaceful retirement seemed no longer to care or wish for this sedative, yet he never lost his pleasure in smoking, and to the last keenly enjoyed his pipe or cigar, the more when he had a friend with him to chat over old times. Merrily would they laugh together as he related some of the interesting reminiscences of his long cathedral career.

He has told how, on one occasion, when the service had been changed to please some visitors, the organ-blower, much offended, said, " You can play Rogers in D if you like, but I shall blow Attwood in C."

And of another, who, having blown the organ for a lay-clerk's trial, applied to the successful candidate for a fee. The gentleman, much surprised, said, " I don't remember you ; what did you do for me ? " The man replied, " Please, sir, I blew you in. "

Speaking of trials, years ago, before pedal-organs were completed, an organ-builder, somewhat in advance of the day, had just added some large pedal-pipes to an instrument in the church he attended. For this he was thought so clever that he was asked to adjudicate at the trial for a new organist. As one after another of the candidates played, the builder seemed dissatisfied, for they did not produce what he considered to be due effect, and he made audible remarks upon their performances.

At last, however, one candidate did make the pipes speak occasionally, and another young man, seeing the pleasure this gave to the all-important judge, stole out of the church, procured some leaden weights, and carefully secreted them until his time for trial came. Then he placed one of them on a bass note, and extemporized to this pedale.

When he wished to modulate, he deftly pushed

the leaden weight on to whichever note was required.

Needless to say, his effort received warm approbation, and he got appointed to the post.

On one occasion some gentlemen of the choir were spending a musical evening together at the house of an admirer, who, although not a musical man, was delighted to show hospitality to such singers of distinction. After supper someone suggested that they should have a part-song entitled, "Would you know my Celia's charms?" The men did their part so admirably, suiting the action to the word, that mine host grew alarmed, and, wishing to pacify the apparently excited singers, rose from his seat, walked round the table, and, patting one of them on the back, said, in most soothing tones, "Come, gentlemen, we've had *such* a pleasant evening together; don't let us end with a quarrel."

CHAPTER XX.

IN March of 1856 a festival service was held in the Wolsey Chapel at Windsor, to celebrate the conclusion of the Crimean War, and a grand performance of the "Creation" was given, under Dr. Elvey's direction.

Later in the year he went down to Tenbury to assist at the opening of the church erected there by Sir Frederick Ouseley.

The Doctor presided at the organ, which he had planned. It was in a very unfinished state, but he was said to have "done wonders" with it, and to have succeeded in demonstrating that the church possessed great acoustic properties.

One of his own anthems, "Almighty and everlasting God," specially composed for the occasion, formed part of the service.

Allusion has been made to the unfinished state of the organ, and the same remark might be applied to the approaches. Owing to the dragging of the materials for the building up a steep hill, and the constant passage of heavily-laden waggons, this had been reduced to such a deplorable state, that on the day appointed for the consecration, after a night's heavy rain, it was some inches deep in mud. Dr. Elvey used to give a lively and graphic description of the dismay of the numerous clergy, who toiled up the hill in procession, or, as he described it, pranced along, endeavouring by holding up their surplices to guard them from contact with the black mud.

Afterwards all the guests (of whom there were an immense number) partook of luncheon "in common," and, said Dr. Elvey, with one of his merry smiles, when alluding to the occasion, "It was *very* common!"

The following summer was a somewhat eventful one for him.

In May, his anthem, "In that Day," was performed at Exeter Hall by the Sacred Harmonic Society, Dr. Elvey himself conducting.

It may be remembered that this anthem was originally composed for the "Festival of the Ancients" in 1850. It was dedicated by special permission to H.R.H. Prince Albert; and a few weeks before the performance at Exeter Hall it was given at Windsor Castle before Her Majesty under Dr. Elvey's direction.

At Exeter Hall it was preceded by a splendid rendering of " The Creation." Upon the anthem the " Times " made the following remarks :

" Mr. Surman gave an interesting performance last night, consisting of Haydn's oratorio, 'The Creation,' and a new anthem by Dr. Elvey, organist of the Chapel Royal, Windsor.

" An original work by an English composer would be sufficiently a matter of interest were it even in a less ambitious school than that to which Dr. Elvey has, in the present instance, directed his attention. The anthem, 'In that Day shall this song be sung,' is modelled in the style of our great Cathedral masters ; . . . it is written with the correctness and purity that spring from a thorough and well-grounded musical education.

" It opens with a short recitative in B flat, which introduces a chorus in the same key, 'Open the gates,' in the fugued style.

" A solo for tenor with choral responses and coda in F, ' Thou wilt keep him in perfect peace,' follows.

" A short chorus in full harmony, in B flat, ' Trust ye in the Lord,' leads to a vigorous choral fugue in the same key, ' For in the Lord Jehovah,' remarkable for good counterpoint and plain melody, and the clever pedal-point on the dominant. The following chorale in G minor, ' Be gracious unto us,' contrasts well with what precedes and comes after it, while its grave tone is in strict keeping with the words.

" A solo for an alto voice, with the chorus, ' The Lord is exalted,' conducts to the final fugue in E flat, ' Amen,' which presents a well-marked theme, dexterously elaborated."

This anthem, it may be mentioned here, together with " I beheld, and lo ! a great multitude," were given to Surman, and though they have since been bought and sold at publishers' sales for considerable sums, Dr. Elvey never received anything for them.

About a month after this performance the old choristers of St. George's held a festive gathering, which appears to have been quite a red-letter day.

It is graphically described as follows : " The old choristers held their ' gathering ' yesterday week at Windsor, and from all accounts appear to have enjoyed a few hours' most agreeable respite from the duties of everyday life.

" The day's proceedings commenced with the morning service at St. George's Chapel, after which the organ was tried, and the merits of the recent additions discussed. Then, having seen the state apartments, the whole party went to Old Windsor in a pleasure-barge. This was a pile which, from being honestly and indisputably the antithesis of your modern new-fangled 'outrigger' style of craft, both in build and speed, might very well have been the identical vessel that used to convey the Saxon kings to the palace at Windles-ofra, the ancient name of Old Windsor. The bargemen (as an architect would say) were certainly 'later insertions,' though even they were not in the 'decorated style.'

" In rather more than two hours—the distance achieved was about two miles—the 'old boys' landed at Old Windles-ofra, where, through the courtesy of Mr. and Mrs. Wrench, at the kind intercession of Dr. Elvey, an excellent cold collation had been laid out in their grounds by 'Mine host of the White Hart hostelrie,' on a lawn sloping down to the river, and shaded by a row of venerable and gigantic trees.

" Dinner being concluded, several toasts were proposed, and many glees sung, and the proceedings of the day were being carried on with great spirit, when it was announced that, in order to catch the last London train, the party must take to the barge immediately.

"This was soon accomplished, and the 'old choristers' returned to New Windsor as quietly as people usually do after dinner. Not many hats were lost, and no lives.

"Seriously, those present experienced such genuine pleasure from meeting their old school companions—to say nothing of the beautiful prospects and excellent cheer enjoyed during the day—that it was proposed that the mere 'gathering' should at once be formed into a 'society,' so that such an annual meeting might in future be relied upon by its metropolitan and provincial members, and looked forward to as one of the pleasant recreations to be participated in during the summer holidays."

On July 21st, a choral festival in aid of the Choir Benevolent Fund was held in St. George's.

The Chapel was crowded with lovers of Cathedral music, and universal satisfaction reigned at the completeness of the performance.

Dr. Elvey's time had been thus fully occupied, but during these summer months he yet found leisure to add another to his already long list of compositions.

This was an anthem, "Sing, O Heavens!" written for the Festival of the Three Choirs, which this year was held at Worcester.

It was a somewhat lengthy work, as the performance of it occupied fully twenty-five minutes.

It consists of six movements, and is scored for a full orchestra.

The anthem seemed to give great satisfaction, for it was much admired, and pronounced by good judges to be one of his ablest compositions.

A critic at the time said:

"The choruses are grand, the subjects of the fugues most impressive, and worked out with consummate skill." Warm praise indeed!

Throughout these years Dr. Elvey worked hard at composition, and it was at this period that he produced many, if not most, of his finest works.

In 1858 he was occupied in writing his anthem, "This is the Day which the Lord hath made," scored for a full band.

It was composed especially for, and used on, the day of thanksgiving appointed after the suppression of the Indian Mutiny, at a special service in St. George's Chapel (May 1st, 1859).

Dr. Elvey selected the words of the opening chorus from a verse in the Psalms beginning with, "This is the Day which the Lord hath made," set to bold and broad phrases; and then a fugue to the words, "We will rejoice and be glad in it." A short larghetto—"A sound of battle"—introduced later on the answering chorus, "But the Lord hath delivered us."

Then comes an elaborate fugue to the words, "Not unto us, O Lord!" wrought out in Sir George's musicianly manner. Perhaps the tenor solo, "O that men would praise the Lord!" might be considered the gem of the anthem, a graceful and taking melody, written with true devotional feeling and pathos.

A semi-chorus, "He maketh peace," is full of repose and beauty.

A return to the first subject and opening sentences brings this interesting work to a close; it contains some of Sir George Elvey's characteristic thoughts, and is the production of a thorough musician and ripe scholar.

A few years before, Elvey composed a morning and evening Cathedral service in F, of which Dr. Crotch, to whom it was dedicated, said that he only wished he could show his approbation in a more serviceable way than by consenting to have his name printed on the title-page.

Throughout his life Sir George was always a great admirer of the then Oxford professor, whom he had known well as a young man in the cathedral city, and it was a source of deep regret to him that the works of one of the most gifted men that England has ever produced should be left unpublished and unknown.

In later years he made great efforts to secure the publication of one of these, an oratorio, "The Captivity of Judah," and induced the Sacred Harmonic Society to give a performance of another entitled "Palestine" at Exeter Hall. He took immense trouble to collect subscriptions to bring out the former of these fine works, and wrote innumerable letters on the subject. Unfortunately, however, he did not succeed in getting the necessary guarantee, although the idea was warmly supported by Sir Sterndale Bennett, Sir Michael Costa, Sir Herbert Oakeley, Sir John Goss, Sir Robert Stewart, Dr. Corfe, and Sir Frederick Ouseley, the latter of whom wrote thus :

"The more I look into the score of ' The Captivity,' the more I like it."

It was the custom for many years for all the

Windsor lay-clerks to be engaged to sing at the
annual festival of the charity children at St. Paul's
Cathedral.

There were very few festivals held, either in
London or in the country, at which Dr. Elvey and
some members, at least, of his choir, were not
present.

At these he frequently acted as conductor, more
especially when one of his own greater works was
performed.

At the invitation of Sir John Goss, he took the
bâton at the meetings held in St. Paul's Cathedral on behalf of the Sons of the Clergy Corporation, which he conducted until 1867, when he
resigned.

On one occasion, when the men were singing in
London, the boys, and three lay-clerks who had
not been engaged, sang the service in the Chapel
instead of saying it, as had generally been done on
these occasions. Dr. Elvey did not like such a
miserably balanced choir, and it was whispered
among the boys after service that there would be
no singing in the afternoon, and that they might
even have a holiday from service altogether ; the
few lay-clerks being considered sufficient to say
the responses and Psalms.

Visions of some pleasant excursion to Virginia Water, or elsewhere, floated before their eyes, but they nevertheless went into school as usual. Presently, however, Canon Anson arrived and said it had been decided to have no singing at the afternoon service; and that he wished the boys to have an excursion up the river at his expense, and Dr. Elvey had volunteered with the master, Mr. Bransom, to take charge of them.

The affair is thus described by one who was then a chorister :

"After an early dinner we started; one boat was rowed by Dr. Elvey and his pupil, Fred Burgiss, the other by Mr. Bransom and two of the biggest boys.

"I (*i.e.* Frost, the author of the account) was among the boys consigned to the care of Dr. Elvey. Away we went up the river, enjoying to the full that glorious June afternoon. I fear the British public was greatly deceived as to our whereabouts, for it was Ascot Cup day, and good Canon Anson was sadly afraid that those who attended the afternoon service would imagine that, as there was no singing, the choir must have gone to the races.

"He therefore had a notice placed at the Chapel

doors, which said : " No choral service : choir at St. Paul's.'

"The Doctor brought Mendelssohn's open-air part-music with him, and this we sang at intervals as we returned home under a bright evening sky.

"At times we had quite an audience following us along the bank, and had more than once to refuse their invitations to disembark and give them an impromptu concert.

CHAPTER XXI.

IN October, 1860, Dr. Elvey received a terrible blow in the death of Dr. Stephen Elvey, his elder brother. The intense devotion of these two to one another is almost impossible to describe. They had so many grounds of union; first and foremost, their deep love for the Saviour, and secondly, their musical tastes and profession, being both employed in the same branch of art.

Dr. Stephen was nearly eleven years George's senior; the younger brother looked up to the elder with a most intense reverence and affection. Even to the close of his life he never mentioned his name without deep pathos in his voice. Dr. Stephen's death was sudden and tragic.

His Sundays at Oxford were a perpetual whirl; for not only was he organist of New College, but choragus of the University, and organist of St. Mary's and St. John's.

In consequence of his lameness and his holding so many appointments, he was obliged to be con-

veyed from pillar to post by the University " gon-
dola," a bath-chair. In hurrying off from one
service to another one Sunday, the attendant took
too close a turn round a corner, and ran against a
Church dignitary. To remove the vehicle from off
his feet, he instinctively dashed out both hands,
throwing its occupant into the road.

Dr. Stephen was a heavy man; the shock proved
too much for him, and he went home to die.

A short account of one who exercised such an
influence over Dr. Elvey, and to whom, to a great
extent, he owed both his musical education and the
moulding of his musical opinions, may not be out
of place here.

Stephen Elvey, born, reared, and to the close of
his life living in a Cathedral city, was strongly
imbued with the influences of the English Cathedral
system.

At the age of seven years he became a chorister
in Canterbury Cathedral, and ever since then he
exercised the profession of Church music, imbued
with the true principles of the English choral
service, and devoting his best energies throughout
his entire life to this ministry and vocation in the
Church, for such we must consider the active
profession of the ecclesiastical musician.

At Canterbury he was a pupil of Mr. Jones, and in 1831 he succeeded at Oxford another young man of promise, Alfred Bennett, who was crushed to death by the overturning of a coach returning from the Worcester Festival. Dr. Elvey had previously lost his right leg by an accidental shot. With a wooden substitute he was enabled to manage the swell, having still the left at liberty for the pedal notes.

Notwithstanding this disadvantage, few performers could give greater effect to Handel's choruses than the organist of New College, aided by a fine instrument in Wykeham's lofty and beautiful chapel.

In 1856 he was appointed choragus in the University of Oxford.

He was well known in his profession as a profound and talented musician, thoroughly versed in the best school of English music.

As an organist he was not only one of those who "found out musical tunes," but in his intelligent and devout understanding of the song of praise he showed that he exercised himself day and night in the law of the Lord, and that the Lord's " testimonies were his delight and his counsellors."

His proficiency and taste will long be remembered, especially by the frequenters of New College Chapel, with which his name was for so many years associated.

In his later years he devoted a great portion of his time and attention to the correct chanting of the Psalms, and in 1856 he published a Psalter pointed upon the soundest and most approved principles. This work was the result of a reverent and thoughtful study of the language and meaning of the Psalms, combined with a very accurate adaptation of the words to the musical divisions.

This Psalter is deservedly in very high repute as the most careful and elaborate work of the kind, and it has exercised much influence in Cathedral and other choirs, by promoting a more exact and intelligent method of chanting. After his death it became the property of his brother George.

Dr. Elvey's knowledge of the Scriptures, especially the words of the Psalms, was remarkable, and his application of them, to the last, instructive and consoling.

His private life was distinguished for kindness and self-sacrificing exertions for others.

He was a true type of what the English Cathedral training can produce and foster; it not only afforded his vocation in life, but he had imbibed that tone and spirit which it should be the effect of such influences to create, that devotional appreciation of the Church's services, and that deep religious feeling which he possessed.

Dr. Stephen Elvey, as those who were acquainted with his inward life knew well, was a man not only of great kindliness and real affectionateness of heart, but of sincere humble piety.

The history of such a man possesses, in some measure, an interest for the musical world at large, for it serves to illustrate that kind of professional life and devotional spirit which the Church of England choral system has produced and should ever foster.

In December, 1861, occurred that which was a grief and a calamity to the nation at large—the death of the beloved Prince Consort. This blow, coming so soon after the death of his brother, was very deeply felt by Dr. Elvey, who grieved much for the loss of the Prince, ever his kind friend and patron. His heart bled sorely for his beloved Queen, into whose grief he could enter, as can only those who have passed through the fiery trial themselves.

It had ever been a great delight to him to serve

the Prince, who in return had always shown a ready appreciation of his talents and abilities.

At the funeral, on December 23rd, in St. George's Chapel, Dr. Elvey played the organ during the mournful service.

As the procession advanced, the commencement of the Burial Service, " I am the Resurrection and the Life, saith the Lord," was sung by the full choir to Dr. Croft's music. At the nave was commenced the passage, " I know that my Redeemer liveth," still sung to Croft's melancholy, dirge-like music, so touching, so inexpressibly mournful in its long, soft cadences.

At the end of the lesson the choir sang the German chorale, " I shall not in the grave remain."

The words of the latter were great favourites of the Prince, and the music for this, as well as for another chorale which followed at a later portion of the service, was composed by Dr. Elvey specially for the occasion.

It is impossible to imagine anything more exquisitely touching than the cadence to the lines :

> " So fall asleep in slumber deep,
> Slumber that knows no ending."

This was chanted by the choir in whispered

tones, that seemed to moan through the building with a plaintive solemnity as deep in its sorrow as the notes of the " Dead March."

A rough translation from the German gives the words of this mournful hymn as follows :

> " I shall not in the grave remain,
> Since Thou death's bonds hast sever'd ;
> By hope with Thee to rise again,
> From fear of death deliver'd.
> I'll come to Thee, where'er Thou art,
> Live with Thee, from Thee never part ;
> Therefore to die is rapture.
> And so to Jesus Christ I'll go,
> My longing arms extending ;
> So fall asleep in slumber deep,
> Slumber that knows no ending,
> Till Jesus Christ, God's only Son,
> Opens the gates of bliss,—leads on
> To Heaven, to life eternal."

*　　　*　　　*　　　*

Again the Dean, the Hon. and Rev. Gerald Wellesley, resumed the service in a strained and broken voice—for all in the Chapel made no attempt to conceal their emotion—with the sublime passage, " Man that is born of woman hath but a short time to live, and is full of misery."

Then was sung, with exquisite pathos, by Mr. Tolley, Martin Luther's hymn, " Great God! what do I see and hear?" After the earth had been thrown upon the coffin, the choir sung, " I heard a voice from Heaven," to Croft's plaintive music ; and after the reading of the prayer, " Almighty God, with whom do live," an English translation was chanted of another of the Prince's favourite chorales, as follows :

> " To Thee, O Lord, I yield my spirit,
>   Who break'st in love this mortal chain ;
> My life I but from Thee inherit,
>   And death becomes my chiefest gain.
> In Thee I live, in Thee I die,
> Content—for Thou art ever nigh."

Then Dr. Elvey commenced the solemn strains of the " Dead March in Saul," as the mourners gathered round to take a last look into the grave ; so deep was the grief which he, as well as all present, felt at the sad and solemn ceremony, that it nearly overcame him, and it was only with a great effort and the utmost difficulty that he could manage to complete the March.

In later years he would often speak of the eager expectation and deep anxiety in which he sat up late, on the last sad evening of the Prince's life, and of the hush of gloom and sorrow that seemed to fill the night when at last the news was brought that he had passed away. He used to say he felt as if he had lost another brother.

For twenty years Dr. Elvey, with infinite pains, prepared the music for the memorial service on each anniversary of the Prince's death.

Perhaps few are aware of the work that this entailed. It was extremely difficult to find suitable music to make sufficient variety on these occasions, and he often found it necessary to compose various pieces himself for the services.

In this way his anthems, "The Souls of the Righteous" and " Blessed are the Dead," were written. As there was no instrument at the Mausoleum (where the service was held after 1869), great care was required in preparing the music. Each member of the choir was provided with a full copy of the service in Sir George's writing, with every mark of expression most carefully inserted, and the writing of these, with the requisite rehearsals, cost him annually at least a fortnight's hard work.

CHAPTER XXII.

ON March 10th, 1863, the royal borough
decked itself in the gayest of holiday attire,
for on that day the heir to the throne was married
to the Princess Alexandra of Denmark.   All the
inhabitants of Windsor strove to show their
delight in that an event of such import to the
nation at large was to be celebrated in their
midst.

Unfortunately the weather, which had hitherto
been lovely and spring-like, to everyone's great disappointment turned cold and wet.   A full description of the gorgeous ceremonial would be foreign
to the purpose of this book, and soon cause it to
exceed the limits of a volume ; but a reference to
the newspapers of that date serves to show the
intense and universal interest excited by the
marriage.

Shortly after eleven on the eventful morning
all was in order.   From the top of the park hill
there looked down on the broad avenue, skirted

by the two lines of household troops, the splendidly-mounted Life Guards, whose cuirasses gleamed like silver in the sunlight. Below the iron gates, and extending on each side to the old arch leading to St. George's Chapel, the Berkshire Volunteers were formed up about 600 strong, under the command of their colonel.

Ranged along the Park front of the Castle, and opposite the grand entrance, were the children of Her Majesty's Schools, about a hundred and twenty in number.

On the towers and turrets of the grand old Castle, on the ramparts which surround the venerable pile, on the mound which forms the base of the imposing tower, over gateways and from windows, and from tall roofs, from every point which afforded a view of the line of procession, the eyes of countless spectators peered expectantly and waited impatiently the first blast of the trumpet that should herald the approach of the royal party.

" As the constant stream of all that is great and noble and worthy in the country swept past on their way to the grand old Chapel of Edward, hallowed by so many associations of chivalrous and knightly deeds, and sacred to so much that is grand or gloomy in past history, the scene was one of continued ever-varying brilliant pageantry."

Dr. Elvey presided at the organ, and took charge of the musical part of the service on the great occasion, for which he had specially composed a wedding anthem, "Sing unto God." The first chorus is an elaborate setting for five voices, who break in, after an instrumental prelude, with a shout, in massive harmonies, to the initial words. The basses and tenors then give out the subject of a fugue, fully developed in all its parts, to the verse, "Sing praises to the Lord." After passing through all the phases of well-constructed imitation, chords are reverted to, and the first subject and words bring this finely-written number to a close.

The next semi-chorus is accompanied by the organ only; this is a quiet and graceful quartet, written in the author's most melodious vein.

The third movement is a "German Chorale," and introduces the wood wind with the organ.

"How happy ye!" Fine bold harmony is set to this verse, which closes on the solo organ.

A short largo, "Lo! thus shall the man be blessed," with full band, serves as an introduction to the last "Amen" chorus. Returning to the fugal form, a grand subject is recited by the basses, answered by all the voices in turn, and considerably enlarged upon; the instrumentation is much heightened in colour, and brings this splendidly-written anthem to a close in truly regal style.

At the ceremony Dr. Elvey wore his robes as a doctor of music. The choir was removed from the rows of benches beneath the canons' stalls in the body of the Chapel which they ordinarily occupy, and a considerable accession to their numbers having been made, both of male and female voices, the choir was placed on the right-hand side of the organ, in the open loft between the nave and the choir. Among the lady vocalists was Madame Jenny Lind Goldschmidt, whose clear voice and pure intonation were easily distinguishable in the chorales of the service.

The organ was supplemented by a complete orchestra, led by Mr. Anderson, the director of Her Majesty's private band.

As the bridegroom's procession advanced, Dr. Elvey played Mendelssohn's march from "Athalie;" and as the lovely bride entered with her bevy of fair maids, Handel's march from "Joseph" was performed.

When they reached the altar, and before the marriage service commenced, a long chorale by H.R.H. the late Prince Consort was sung by the choir.

At the end of the first blessing, the 67th Psalm was chanted, and at the conclusion of the service the Hallelujah chorus from Beethoven's " Mount of Olives " was sung before the bride and bridegroom retired.

*   *   *   *   *

A year or two afterwards, when Dr. Elvey was a guest at the Prince of Wales's garden party, he was much gratified at being warmly thanked by His Royal Highness for the anthem he had composed for his wedding. The Prince of Wales was always a very kind friend to Dr. Elvey, and the latter was much touched by his thoughtfulness and consideration at a time when most people would have been too much engaged to remember and be grateful for actions performed for them so long before.

To the close of his life Dr. Elvey always spoke with pleasure of a delightful visit he made to Lord Antrim in Ireland about this time.

He had an extremely rough passage across, and the steamer was forced to remain all night at sea.

This, however, he thoroughly enjoyed, as he was an excellent sailor, and appeared on the water to lose his nervousness. The following day he arrived very tired and travel-worn at Lord Antrim's hospitable house. After dinner, his host, noticing how fatigued he was, suggested that perhaps he would like to retire to rest.

That night he never forgot, for the effect of the sea air was so soporific that he used laughingly to declare he had never had such a sleep in his life.

Here he had great fun, and probably contributed not a little to the enjoyment of his fellow-guests, for he was ever the soul of a party, and exerted himself greatly to give pleasure, especially to young people.

His violin was his constant companion when visiting among friends, for he played so beautifully that they always begged him to bring this instrument with him. Although he much objected to play for people to hear how he played, he was always delighted to do so to give pleasure to any friends who really wished for some music.

As an instance of his ready wit the following anecdote may be related :

Whilst staying with some friends in the country, he, with a large party, went for a picnic, taking his violin with him. When luncheon was all ready on the grass, several friends of the name of Lamb were nowhere to be found.

At this Dr. Elvey whipped out his violin and played, to the immense amusement of all, "Little Bopeep, she lost her sheep."

On another occasion, after being introduced to an engaged couple, he quietly crept to the piano, and in a moment the merry strains of "Haste to the Wedding" rang through the room, causing much merriment to the assembled company, but somewhat discomforting the bashful pair.

Another funny anecdote is related by one of his pupils, who says :

"I have before me a slip of paper sent into my room when I was practising 'Blow in A' from Boyce's score.

"It runs thus : 'I like Blow as well as anyone, but I can't stand him at dinner-time. Blowed if I can !'"

At this time, and indeed until the Cloisters were rebuilt, Dr. Elvey's pupils, as may be seen from the above story, had a practising room in his house, and this was sometimes rather a trial, as the following incident serves to show :

"I recollect," says a pupil, "that I was practising

some exercises in his house before eight in the morning. Presently the door opened, and he came running in, evidently in the middle of shaving, and said, ' My good sir, you have nearly made me cut myself; you *will* play a wrong note there.' "

On April 20th, 1865, Dr. Elvey married Miss Jarvis, having been two years before left a widower with four little children, the youngest only three weeks old.

This year he was asked to accept the post of musical examiner at Oxford, which he did, although he never cared much for the work of an examiner, as he felt so keenly for those who were defeated.

In speaking of examinations, he would often relate the tale of a young man who had to go before Dr. Crotch. Upon being requested to play an organ solo, he selected the anthem known to all Cathedral choirs as, " Be Merciful "— CROTCH.

CHAPTER XXIII.

THE following year (1866) Dr. Elvey was again busy with a royal ceremonial — the marriage of H.R.H. Princess Helena to Prince Christian, which took place in the private chapel of the Castle on the 5th of July.

Not long after this event, Dr. Elvey lost his very kind friend, Mr. William Whitbread, to whom he was much attached.

He had often stayed with him in his home, and on one of these occasions his host presented him with a very beautiful and valuable snuff-box, which had once belonged to Frederick the Great.

Mr. Hancock, a favoured chorister, whom he took with him, by request, to Southill, thus describes one of these pleasant visits :

" When staying with Dr. Elvey at Mr. Whitbread's house, I was invited (with my fellow-chorister) to join the house-party in a day's shooting. But the Doctor was aghast at the idea of our carrying guns (as well he might be) ; weapons of all kinds were a source of horror to him, and he would never have them near him if he could avoid it. Great, indeed, was his discomfort when obliged to wear his sword, and nothing of this kind, not even his razors, would he permit to remain in his bedroom.

"Only after much persuasion did he consent to our following the party with the game-cart. Even then he was uneasy about us, and appeared quite surprised and almost disappointed at our returning to the house as sound as when we left it.

"I well remember, too, that he was thrown into a great state of trepidation at the commencement of this visit; for we had to get from Paddington to Euston Station in a great hurry, and, the morning being very frosty and the roads slippery, our cab-horse fell in the Euston Road.

"The shock which we received by the sudden stoppage of the vehicle; the necessity for our changing rapidly into another cab; to say nothing of the effects of the inevitable crowd which assembled, all combined to throw Dr. Elvey into such a condition of excitement that he had hardly recovered his nerve when we reached our destination in Bedfordshire.

"But, once there, I think he was as merry as I

ever knew him.   A large party of guests were in the house, but he showed nothing of his usual timidity when in the midst of strangers.

" He was often asked to perform on a chamber organ which our host had placed in one of the rooms, and I noticed that he almost invariably included in his programme an extempore fantasia on the ' Vicar of Bray.'   Whether it was his own choice, or that he knew it to be a favourite air of Mr. Whitbread's, I cannot say, but I do not remember his playing it on any other occasion.

" During this visit a skating party was organized one morning.   Needless to say, Dr. Elvey did not venture to trust himself on skates, but he insisted upon going down to the lake with the other guests, and I presently found him, seated on a chair, and hitching himself along the edge of the ice.

" He declined my offer to ' push behind,' and declared he was enjoying himself greatly, and he evidently was.

" On many other occasions when I went from Windsor with him, I was forcibly struck by his unwonted mirth and cheerfulness.   One was tempted to forget the master and teacher, and to remember only the kind and genial friend."

*   *   *   *   *

For several years the Doctor held a large music-class at his house, which in 1868 was developed into the "Windsor and Eton Madrigal Society," started by him, with the assistance of Mr. Bliss and several other gentlemen, for the practice and private performance of madrigals and other un-accompanied part-music, secular and sacred.

This society was very successful, and started the first season with eighty-seven performing members and forty-eight non-performers.

These numbers continued steadily to increase until, when Sir George retired from his honorary conductorship in 1882, the performing members numbered considerably over a hundred.

The first concert of the society was held on December 5th, 1868, and was a very successful one.

For these concerts Sir George composed several pieces ; among others, " The Zetland Fishermen," " Softly, softly, blow, ye breezes," " Hark ! those voices," " Shall I wasting in despair," " Love under friendship's vesture," " Bright may the sun shine o'er him," written for the birthday of H.R.H. the Prince of Wales, 1868.

For a Shakespeare concert, arranged in February, 1882, he wrote his song, "Caliban."

" All Sir George Elvey's compositions, anthems, and part-songs," says Mr. Rootham, "have this feature most clearly marked, they are so 'singable;' not a single note in any of the parts—treble, alto, tenor, or bass, that is not easy of production. This makes it a real pleasure to vocalists to take part in any of his compositions, as they afford a fair opportunity of showing the various voices at their best.   I suppose that there is scarcely a tenor lay-clerk in the kingdom who does not feel it to be a real pleasure to sing the solo part in 'In that Day;' and so with all his compositions, there is something real and substantial in them all.   In fact, they were the reflex of the man himself."

In the summer of 1868 Dr. Elvey went into the Lake District for his holiday.

He was passionately fond of fine scenery, and intensely enjoyed the lovely country around Ambleside and Keswick.

He made many excursions in the district, visiting Furness, Grange, and the beautiful old church of Cartmell, where he sat down to try the organ, and not a little astonished the old sexton, who had never before heard such exquisite strains proceed from the old instrument.

Whilst taking a trip by steamer on Lake Windermere one day, he was astonished to hear a young man on the boat playing the cornet very beautifully, and, entering into conversation with him, he became much interested, and determined, if possible, to help him into a better position. Upon his return to Windsor he recommended him to the colonel and bandmaster of the 1st Life Guards, who gladly availed themselves of his services, and were delighted to find that his playing surpassed even what they had been led to expect from Dr. Elvey's recommendation.

Unfortunately, after he had been for some time a member of the band, he was recognized as a deserter, which grave offence he had committed through fear of being a second time sent to India.

The man was obliged to return at once to the regiment from which he had deserted, and undergo the necessary punishment for his offence, to the great grief of the bandmaster, and of the poor man himself.

As soon as his term of imprisonment was completed, Dr. Elvey left no stone unturned to obtain his discharge and reinstatement in his former position. This cost him endless work and trouble for months, but at last he was allowed to buy the soldier's discharge.

This man, unlike many, proved himself well worthy of the trouble taken, and with the first money he could contrive to get together he repaid his benefactor the sum he had advanced to buy him off.

This was only one of many instances of disinterested kindness shown by Dr. Elvey to those who casually crossed his path.

Those who had the most intimate acquaintance with him could not fail to be impressed by the great tenderness of his disposition ; his sympathy with anyone in trouble was of the deepest and most sincere kind. Like the Master whom he served, he truly wept with those who wept, and rejoiced with those that did rejoice.

He was constantly made the recipient of various sad tales, as all who knew him were sure of his keen sympathy with them, and of his ready help.

Although his means were far from large, he never willingly refused one appeal for assistance, but gave ungrudgingly to the utmost of his power. Like all who occupy a public position, he was frequently exposed to much unkindness and annoyances of various kinds, but he never complained, and readily forgave those who wronged him, and, as occasion offered, was ever the first to render them help when required.

" I remember," writes an old pupil, " one man in particular making himself very obnoxious. In course of time this man fell ill and died, and there was no one who made more frequent inquiries, and did more for his comfort during his illness, than the Doctor. After his death, he was the means of starting a subscription for the widow who was left penniless, and thus enabled her to pay all that was due, and to have a little in hand to start on her own account."

*　　*　　*　　*　　*

One of the gentlemen of his choir thus writes of him :

" We always looked upon Sir George as a friend to whom we could go in any trouble or difficulty.

" If we were preparing for a concert or private engagement, we could take our music to him and he never failed to give us his most ready and willing help ; indeed, he would take as great pains in practising such pieces as he would have done had he himself been responsible for their performance."

CHAPTER XXIV.

DURING the time that Dr. Elvey was at Windsor, he constantly took his choir to the Castle to serenade different members of the royal family on their birthdays, or for other musical entertainments.

He often used to laugh over one of the early morning concerts, when the choir went up to the rooms of the Crown Princess of Prussia. It was in November, and as the affair was fixed for 7 a.m. the day had scarcely broken when the men crept quietly to their allotted positions. Added to this, it was pouring with rain, and the light was just sufficient to show that the Long Walk was almost under water, but utterly inadequate for anyone to see a note of music. As if in irony of the unpropitious elements, the first piece on the programme was " Hail! Smiling Morn" (Spofforth).

This would probably, under the circumstances, have been dispensed with, but for the fact that the light being so bad the singers were dependent on what they all knew by heart.

On April 15th, 1872, Sir George went with the choir to serenade the Princess Beatrice on her birthday. For this occasion he wrote a part-song, "The Thorn is in the bud," which was very much admired both by the Queen and Princess Beatrice. In the evening he received the following letter from Dean Wellesley:

" DEAR SIR GEORGE,

" I have a more than usually flattering message to you from the Queen. 'Tell Sir George Elvey how pleased the Queen was with the singing to-day, and how much she admired the piece composed for Princess Beatrice, with such pretty verses.'

" Yours sincerely,
(Signed) " G. WELLESLEY."

With these concerts Sir George took unlimited trouble, never allowing one to take place without a rehearsal, however late the request might reach him.

Sometimes the choir was summoned to his house between 10.30 and 12 p.m., or, more frequently still, at 6.30 a.m., to rehearse before the serenade.

As he thus spared no pains to make the performances satisfactory, it was very gratifying to him to hear frequently from Her Majesty's own lips how pleased she was with the music, and how greatly she admired the singing of his choir.

The last of these occasions on which he conducted was in 1881, when the choir went up to serenade the Duke and Duchess of Connaught. As it was Sunday morning the programme was composed exclusively of sacred music.

Towards the end of 1870, extensive alterations were commenced in the Cloisters. The ground was lowered six feet, and the houses, which were covered with white lath-and-plaster work, and had fallen into a very dilapidated state, were thoroughly repaired and restored to their former condition.

Dr. Elvey's house shared in the general renovation, and considerable additions and alterations were made to it.

This obliged his removal until the work was accomplished, and, somewhat to his discomfort, he and his family resided for a year or two in Clarence Crescent, and subsequently, for a short time, in Eton.

In 1871, Windsor was again gay with a royal wedding. The 21st of March was the day appointed for the marriage of H.R.H. the Princess Louise with the Marquis of Lorne.

Previously to the event Dr. Elvey had paid a short visit to Ascot, and there busily prepared his popular " Festal March " for its first performance. This is a distinct composition, and not, as has been on more than one occasion erroneously stated, taken from any other work.

"Soon after the guests had assembled in St. George's Chapel, and the clergy had ranged themselves to the right and left, the organ of the Chapel seemed to start from watchfulness and rolled forth the first notes of a noble Festal March, the composition of the accomplished organist, Dr. Elvey. There is heard without, another screed of bagpipes, and the bridegroom immediately makes his appearance, accompanied by his supporters.

*　　*　　*　　*　　*

" He gazes steadfastly at the door, the drums outside rattle the salute, the organ rolls forth Mendelssohn's grand march in ' Athalie,' and to the beautiful music paces in the fair central group of all this grandeur and state, the bride and bridesmaids.　Her Majesty the Queen is walking at the side of her daughter, herself being attended by the Prince of Wales and the Duke of Saxe-Coburg.

The Princess advances to the altar, and kneels, as Her Majesty does also, mother and daughter for a moment praying together.

" Then, when they have risen, the nuptial service commences.

*   *   *   *   *

" Then they kneel together, man and wife, and as they rise, the sonorous waves of that lovely organ peal again into the air, a tender and pathetic, but most royal, musical blessing of Beethoven, admirably rendered by Dr. Elvey, and more expressive of the thought and prayers of those witnessing the spectacle than any words could well be.   The voices of the Queen's choristers mingle with the organ with admirable effect.

*   *   *   *   *

" The happy pair lead the way down the crimson path ; the Queen and the Heir-apparent come after the wedded couple, the Duke of Saxe-Coburg keeping his place close by Her Majesty.

"What a different scene was this to those blood-won triumphs from which the German Prince had just come, and how different from the battle-music which he has been hearing, the sweet and holy melody of Handel, with which the skilful organist concludes the ceremony.   Again one is sensible that music is much more eloquent than language."

The day following the royal wedding, Dr. Elvey left Windsor for a very brief holiday after all the work and excitement that had fallen to his share, and when he returned was met at the station by one of his pupils.   Upon inquiring what news there was in Windsor, to his surprise he received the reply, " The news is that you are to be knighted."

On the Friday (March 24th), he, with Dr. W. Sterndale Bennett and Mr. Julius Benedict, went to the Castle to receive from Her Majesty's own hands the honour conferred upon them.

Whilst waiting in the ante-room, they discussed Mozart's additional accompaniments to the " Messiah," and this conversation was such a pleasure to Sir George, that on his return home, when asked about the ceremony, he only remarked with regard to it that he had been afraid of tripping up with his sword, and then enlarged on his discourse with the two brother-musicians, and how greatly delighted he was to find that they both agreed with him that the accompaniments, clever and beautiful as they undoubtedly are, nevertheless are quite out of character with Handel's work.

This conversation had evidently impressed him far more than the regal ceremony, for he never cared to be placed in a position of prominence, and was averse to making an unnecessary display of his honours.

Once, when putting away the box which contained his court uniform, a friend remarked that he had never seen him wearing it. He replied, " No, and I hope you never may ! "

On the Sunday afternoon following the wedding, it was known that a portion of the music used at this ceremonial was to be performed, and an immense congregation filled the choir and nave of St. George's Chapel, the majority having to stand throughout the service. A small band, led by Mr. Gunness, was in the organ-loft, and the trumpeter was Mr. T. Harper. T.R.H. Prince and Princess Christian were present at the service, which was brought to a close with Sir George Elvey's " magnificent " Festal March.

Soon after this the committee of the Windsor and Eton Madrigal Society suggested to the members that they should give a concert in Sir George's honour, the programme for which was to be entirely composed of selections from his works. This idea was warmly taken up, a first-rate band was engaged, and no effort was spared to make the affair a success.

The concert took place in St. Mark's School on the 5th of July, the following being the programme :

PART I.

SACRED CANTATA—"The Lord is King."
Composed for the Gloucester Festival, 1853.

SELECTION FROM A SACRED CANTATA—"Sing unto God."
Performed at the Worcester Festival, 1857.

PART II.

A SELECTION FROM A MS. CANTATA—"Mount Carmel."

SELECTION FROM THE ORATORIO—"The Resurrection and Ascension."

FESTAL MARCH.
Performed at the marriage of H.R.H. Princess Louise,
March 21st, 1871.

CANTATA.
Composed for Her Majesty's birthday.

The following account of the concert has been published :

" The Windsor and Eton Amateur Madrigal Society, at their last grand orchestral concert, testified their high appreciation of the great musical ability of their honorary conductor, Sir George

Elvey, Mus. Doc. Oxon., by making up the whole of their programme from his works.

"The first piece was written for the Gloucester Festival of 1853, and contains some excellent contrapuntal writing, and some elegant solos for soprano, tenor, and bass voices, which were given with adequate effect by Miss Edith Wynne, Mr. W. H. Cummings, Mr. Ramsbottom, and Mr. Orlando Christian. The scoring is thoughtful and good, and the choruses broad and well-written. The second item, 'The Lord will comfort Zion,' was only a selection from a large work composed for the Worcester Festival of 1857; but the portions selected were sufficient to show the scholarship of the composer in the most advantageous light. The contralto solo, sung by Miss Marion Severn, and the three choruses are admirable specimens of Sir George Elvey's style of treatment, and were enthusiastically received. Miss Edith Wynne and Miss Severn sang the two solos from 'Mount Carmel,' with artistic taste; the air, 'Mine eye runneth down,' for contralto, having a beautiful melody, with an elegant clarionet obligato part played by Mr. Webb, and the airs from the oratorio, 'The Resurrection and Ascension,' were brilliantly sung by Mr. Cummings.   These airs are beautiful specimens of thoughtful writing, and bear evidence of the well-used skill of the musician.   The 'Festal March,' which followed, was composed for, and performed at the marriage of Her Royal Highness the Princess Louise, bold, clever, and modern in style, aptly instrumented, and with a vein of fresh melody running through the march, as well for the construction as for the performance, gave great pleasure to the audience.   In the cantata composed for Her Majesty's birthday, Sir George Elvey has treated the 'National Anthem' in a variety of ways, and always cleverly and effectively, as a chorale, as a fugue, and as a fantasia. There is also a well-written madrigal, 'Through the Realm,' introduced into the cantata, and although not so well sung as the other portions of the work, was still enough to show the versatility of the composer's talent.   Sir George Elvey conducted the whole performance; there was an efficient band and chorus, the former led by Mr. Carrodus, and the latter was made up from members of the society under whose auspices the concert was given, together with some past and present pupils of Sir George Elvey; and included also the services of Lady Harrington, Hon. Mrs.

Wellesley, Hon. Mrs. Ponsonby, Hon. Miss Grosvenor, Misses Montresor, Miss Fawkes, Mrs. Ellison, Miss Ellison, Mrs. Hale, Miss De Rosen, Miss F. Fawkes, Sir John Harrington, Mr. Verrinder, Mus. Bac., Mr. Keeton, Mus. Bac., Rev. L. G. Hayne, Mus. Doc., Rev. Thomas Helmore, Rev. H. Snow, Rev. F. F. Vidal, Rev. W. H. Bliss, Mr. H. A. Chignell, Mr. Blair Oliphant, the Hon. Seymour Egerton, and many others. Her Royal Highness the Princess Christian was present among the audience to do honour to Sir George Elvey, and the Rev. Lord Wriothesley Russell, Sir Thomas and Lady Biddulph, Lady Susan Melville, Colonel Howard Vyse, Rev. S. Hawtrey (by whose permission the meeting was held in the schoolroom of St. Mark's), Dr. Fairbank, Mr. John Goss, Mr. Turle, and others, also testified by their presence the desire to pay a well-deserved compliment to Sir George Elvey."

*   *   *   *   *

Sir George, finding it impossible to personally express his thanks to the many friends who had united in giving him such an ovation, well-deserved as it was, shortly afterwards issued the following circular :

"*July 5th*, 1871.

"Sir George Elvey desires to express his heart-felt thanks to all who have, either as performers or audience, assisted in this evening's concert. They may well believe it is an occasion that he can never forget, or cease to remember with deep gratification and pleasure so long as he lives, connected as it is with the honour which Her Majesty has been graciously pleased recently to bestow upon him, and with the Society, in whose service he has spent many happy hours.

"He trusts that all concerned will accept this method of conveying his sense of their kindness, which leaves him but one regret—that he is so little capable of expressing the feelings by which he is so deeply moved."

Whilst staying at Sunninghill in the summer of this year, he wrote his lovely "Gavotte for Violin and Piano," to play at the Hon. Victoria Grosvenor's annual concert at Rickmansworth. On these occasions she generally called upon her old friend and master to play a violin solo.

On his return from one of his many visits to Moor Park, his friends were surprised to hear that Miss Grosvenor had induced him to venture out on horseback with her. This was a wonderful thing for him to do, for he was far too nervous to care to trust himself in such an exalted position.

When a new organ was erected in Rickmansworth Church, Sir George drew up the specification, and took great interest in the work, afterwards going down to take part in celebrating the opening. He was very frequently called upon to preside at the opening of new organs erected in the churches of his friends and pupils. His skilled manipulation and extensive knowledge of effect in the combination of stops greatly enhanced the reputation of any organ-builder.

Amongst those he opened were : Martock, in Somersetshire, Henley-on-Thames, Windsor Parish Church, Eton College, Ealing, Watford, Ascot, Wokingham, Sunningdale, the Royal Holloway College, and Brocklesby, Lincolnshire. In fact, all over the country his well-known skill was frequently requisitioned.

Not long before Sir George left Windsor, he went to open an organ in a town not far from London. As he was standing in the church before taking his place at the instrument, a gentleman was heard to remark, " Sir George Elvey looks rather old ; do you think he can be physically capable of such a performance as we have been led to expect?"

Long ere the service ended, all his doubts were dispelled, and with intense delight he exclaimed, " Marvellous! truly marvellous! I never heard so splendid an accompanist in my life!"

CHAPTER XXV.

IN March, 1874, H.R.H. the Duke of Edinburgh was married to the Grand Duchess Marie of Russia at St. Petersburg.

A few weeks later they reached England, and Windsor was *en fête* to give them a fitting reception.

On the Sunday afternoon following the arrival of the bridal pair at the Castle, notice was duly given that they would attend the service in St. George's Chapel, and a tremendous crowd assembled outside each door long before the clock chimed the hour for opening.

One present thus describes the scene : " I went, long before the doors were opened, to wait at the north entrance, hoping to secure a seat in the Chapel. The crush was terrible, and, as a verger opened the door, I narrowly escaped having my arm broken, and was carried off my feet backwards almost into the middle of the nave.

" I succeeded at last in entering the choir, but as the vergers had neglected to guard the doors every seat was full, and the centre so packed that people could scarcely move hand or foot.

" I managed to make my way out through the lay-clerks' stalls, and, by the kindness of Sir George Elvey, at length found a safe refuge in the organ-loft.

" The sight from this point was extraordinary ; the choir was filled with a living mass, so closely packed that they were unable to stir.   Both vergers were imprisoned among the people, and when the Duke and Duchess arrived (the latter apparently greatly alarmed at the crush), they found their stalls locked, and the vergers, in spite of frantic efforts, made to the serious peril of those around them, were unable to get near to open them.

" In despair, the Duke's equerry held his stick above the heads of the people to receive the bunch of keys, and thus was enabled to admit the royal party to their stalls.

" Besides the Duke and Duchess, there were present Her Majesty the Queen, who, with the Prince and Princess of Wales, occupied the royal closet.   " The Princess Christian, Prince Leopold, and the Lords and Ladies-in-Waiting, were in the stalls of the Knights of the Garter.

"The choir was augmented by some of the choristers of Westminster Abbey and the Chapel Royal, St. James's. Sir George presided at the organ, and he had, in addition, a full string band in the organ-loft, composed of members of Her Majesty's private band, and the band of the 2nd Life Guards, led by Mr. Gunness. The anthem was, "Sing unto God;" and after the service the Russian national hymn was performed, followed by the "Festal March," and concluding with the English national anthem.

Magnificently was the music performed; splendid, indeed, was Sir George's playing on the lovely old organ, the tones of which can never be forgotten by those who heard them, so rich, so full, so sweet, shown off to the greatest advantage by the grand, full style in which he used to play.

For him to play a wrong note or make a mistake of any kind was practically unknown, for nothing was ever left to chance.

On this matter a friend writes: "I well remember noticing, from the time of my first coming to Windsor until his resignation, the great care Sir George always bestowed upon every detail of his work. He would never permit the slightest mistake or inaccuracy to pass at rehearsal, or in either manuscript or printed copies of music in the use of the choir. Everything was well rehearsed, and nothing was left to chance.

"But this fact, above and beyond all, shone out clear and bright—the more so, probably, because it was never obtrusive—that the composer, the organist, the precentor, was not taking part in a mere musical performance, all his efforts being to the praise and glory of God.

"Although engaged for so large a portion of his life in the rendering of the Cathedral Service, it never became to him a cold and formal ordeal. His interest in divine service *as* a service was acute, and no member of the congregation at St. George's could have followed the lessons with closer attention than he. Frequently would he comment upon such passages of Scripture as appealed most strongly to him, and he had a special affection for the prophetical books of the Old Testament and the Book of Job.

"A metaphor used by the prophet Isaiah impressed him very greatly; it was 'As the shadow of a great rock in a weary land.' The example of so amiable and upright a character can never be lost upon the many choristers and pupils who came under his influence. He rests from his labours, and his works follow him."

CHAPTER XXVI.

THE Rev. Lord Wriothesley Russell, who was appointed a Canon of Windsor in 1844, was ever a warm friend to Sir George, who spent many happy hours with him, both at Windsor and at Chenies. Their hearts were so entirely united in the one true bond of fellowship, the love of Christ, that their mutual intercourse was a source of pleasure and profit to both.

Lord Russell, when in residence, often held interesting Gospel meetings for the soldiers, and none enjoyed these more keenly than Sir George, who, with his pupils, never willingly omitted attending them, although at times his gravity was sorely tried during the hymns by the extraordinary vocal sounds from those present.

He also delighted to attend similar meetings for the villagers, held every Wednesday evening during the winter months in the barn at Buckhurst Park, Sunninghill, and many who were then present will remember his devout and earnest face, as he sat drinking in with joy the message of salvation delivered by the late Sir Stevenson Blackwood, Mr. (now the Rev.) Neville Sherbrooke, and others; and he contributed not a little to the enjoyment of those present by playing the harmonium. He took great interest in the choir, trained by the Misses Savory, and was ever ready to write or arrange tunes for them.

A clergyman, writing at this time to a friend, thus speaks of him : "Sir George is an old friend of mine. I have the highest regard for his personal character, which is so gloriously *honest* in these days of humbug and hypocrisy."

In April, 1874, Sir George's oratorio, "The Resurrection and Ascension," was performed by the St. George's Choral Union at the Queen's Hall, Glasgow, and met with marked approval. We cannot refrain from quoting from a full description which was printed with the book of words for the occasion.

After going through each movement it concludes thus :

"So ends a work replete with the most scholarly writing, the most tasteful and elegant melodial designs, the most genuine impulse of a poetical nature, with a dignified and yet tender expression of the purest and most exalted Christian sentiment."

Referring to the final chorus, the " Hallelujah," in this oratorio, Sir F. Ouseley observed, that, after Handel's " Hallelujah," there was no better setting to those words.

In the May following the royal wedding the Czar came over to visit Her Majesty, and during his stay in England a grand performance was given at the Crystal Palace in his honour, by the London contingent of the Handel Festival Choir, and ten military bands, under the direction of Mr. Auguste Manns.

After the Russian March and Hymn, and two or three other pieces, vocal and instrumental, Sir George's "Festal March" was played in grand style by the united bands, to the thorough satisfaction of the composer, who was present.

A much less imposing concert was given shortly after at Datchet under Sir George's conductorship, one piece in the programme being Haydn's "Surprise Symphony." Just before this commenced, Mr. Blair Oliphant, seeing many friends among the performers, said to Sir George, " Cannot you give me something to do ? "

At this Sir George took up a handful of fire-irons, handing them to him, saying, "You can clash these when I give you a signal." A few bars before the appointed place for the discharge, he looked round to see whether his friend was in readiness. This movement was, however, mistaken for the signal, and the "surprise" being promptly given, effectually startled both orchestra and audience.

This year (1874) the series of special Christmas services in St. George's Chapel was commenced. They were an immense enjoyment to all who were able to take part in them, and the following account will give some idea of their beauty :

"It having been announced that a selection from the ' Messiah ' was to be given on Christmas Eve at St. George's Chapel, a large audience assembled and completely filled the vast edifice. They were greatly enraptured and impressed with the harmonious numbers of Handel, and of Sir John Goss and Sir George Elvey.

" Sir George made the magnificent organ speak with its wonted sweetness and power.

"The service opened by the choir singing the Rev. A. Gurney's carol, ' Come ye lofty, come ye lowly,' set to music by Sir George Elvey. Alternate verses were sung by the trebles, altos, and basses, with full choruses. The effect was grand. Selections from Handel's 'Messiah' took the place of the anthem. The freshness of the boys' voices, and their excellent training, never showed itself to greater advantage than in the solos entrusted to them in this instance.

"Of the selected choruses we can speak with unqualified praise, the 'Hallelujah' especially, evidently creating a marked effect upon the audience.

"To Sir George Elvey we are not only indebted for the successful conduct of a service more than ordinarily acceptable, but likewise for an accompaniment to Handel's masterpiece which we but rarely meet with."

The Christmas services satisfactorily ended, Sir George would become the life of the party at home, and with merry jokes and funny tales would make the Christmas evening a time of immense enjoyment to all privileged to be present.

About this time the restoration of the Cloisters was completed, and Sir George was once more comfortably settled in his old house, which was no little satisfaction to him, after being moved from pillar to post for two or three years.

The unsatisfactory state of the chimes in the Curfew Tower near by, had long been a source of

THE CLOISTERS.

Sir George Elvey's House.

Sir George Elvey's Burial-place.

annoyance to him, and with his usual perseverance he devoted a great deal of time and attention to the work of finding out what tune they ought to play. He carefully examined the chime-barrel, and found that several pegs were missing.

These he had supplied; the result being that the tune was rendered intelligible. However, in consequence of the dilapidated state of the works, the performance was far from perfect.

In 1874, under his direction, Mr. Willoughby repaired and restored them, and they now play admirably. It is almost unnecessary to add that the tune played is St. David's, usually sung to the 1st Psalm, "How blest the man who ne'er consents," followed by what is known to bell-ringers as the "King's Change."

THE PAST AND PRESENT STATE OF THE CHIMES.

Both clock and chimes were made about the year 1690, by John Davis, a name well known to readers of Windsor history. This clever workman was the son of one William Davis, blacksmith both to the King and the Corporation. The latter was an ardent royalist. He had executed various works at Windsor Castle in the reign of Charles I.; but, when patronized by Oliver Cromwell, this independent man, though he continued to do the Castle business for the sake of the veneration in which he held that edifice, would not touch a shilling of the usurper's money in return.

John Davis's supply of the clock and chimes for the Curfew Tower is to be found in the records of the Castle. This entry quaintly puts it that John

Davis is to supply the requisite machinery, but that the price to be paid for the same is to be fixed by Sir Christopher Wren, who thus would seem to have added campanology to his many other acquirements.

CHAPTER XXVII.

LIKE all Cathedral churches, St. George's Chapel possessed some peculiar characters, foremost among whom was a man, Billy Leggett by name, who for fifty years regularly attended the daily services. This remarkable man was not merely famous in his own neighbourhood, but, one might almost say, throughout the country.

Eton boys knew "Silly Billy" well, and, in former times, teased him often. Some of our present statesmen, and many of the nobility probably remember him.

Billy made himself chiefly famous by his attendance at the daily services in St. George's Chapel and in Eton College Chapel. At least half a century before his death he began his queer freaks.

His great affection was for the Church, his terrible hatred for the devil. He always spoke of the latter as *him*, and constantly made his horrors a theme for threat and inquiry.

He was unable to read or write, yet could follow

well the morning and evening services, knew the proper collects and lessons for the day, and could parrot-like repeat the Psalms.

He had a reserved seat in each chapel. The Canons of St. George's provided for him in cold weather a mat whereon to stand until the chapel had been warmed. He was usually in attendance some time before the service began, and at times would astonish strangers by talking to himself in the interim. He would frighten anyone who unwittingly stole his seat, for he would stand by and annoy the intruder by making all kinds of grimaces, at the same time giving forth utterances decidedly expressive. Were the wrong lesson read or the wrong collect used, the offending minor canon was sure to suffer; for, though usually quiet when left alone, Billy has been known to spring from his seat in such a case and cry: "That's wrong!" On one Christmas afternoon, indeed, when a minor canon walked to the lectern in St. George's, and made this mistake with regard to a lesson, Billy rushed up to him, seized him by the surplice, told him in a shout of his error, named the proper lesson, and was perfectly indignant because the minor canon would not take his word without going back to the stall to assure himself.

Once the old man was less flurried, but a little more cunning. A minor canon read the wrong collect, and after service evaded Billy, but met him next day, and hoping to pacify him, said at once, "Oh! I've an old waistcoat to give you, and if you'll come to my lodgings I'll let you have it." Billy went, quietly secured the waistcoat, and then turned short upon the giver, "You read the wrong collect last night!"

He was critical also as to the music, had a singular ear-knowledge of it, would join in it when he liked it, and would occasionally make himself somewhat disagreeable in the organ-loft and elsewhere by his more than audible broken tenor quiver-and-quake Amens at the end of the collects or prayers.

He had a perfect notion of what was and what was *not* the correct thing in the way of anthems for certain seasons, feasts, and fasts, and with a little management would give the leading parts of anthems that were wont to be sung on certain days thirty or forty years before.

His memory, in truth, was so good that he would name the particular days of the month for each of such items.

He never failed, either, to compare the ancient

with the modern in music, called the latter "stuff," and, queerly enough, always gave to the ladies the credit of the degenerated taste.

At times, whenever the choir had gone to St. Paul's or elsewhere, he regarded himself as being fully responsible in their absence, and, sitting in his old place, would send forth crooked "Amens" in a voice that seemed a special union of treble, alto, tenor, and bass.

But his weakest point was his aversion to the devil. A passing reference to *him* in the sermon, distinct or otherwise, would cause the old man to gnash his teeth, clasp his hands, and become marvellously excited. He seemed in this matter to have an inner sight and the fullest imagination, for he often fancied he saw *him* perched on the organ, and would openly wonder what would be the organist's words and feelings had he caught the sight. He would occasionally ask Sir George, "You wouldn't like to meet *him* on the organ-loft stairs, would you?"

Hearing of a murder, too, he would say, "Oh, yes, th' old un's bin at it! It's all *him!*"

He always made inquiry on a Monday if the preacher on the day before had run *him* down and given it *him* well, and never failed to seize Sir

George or others who might have been away on a visit to any of our cathedrals, and ask, " Did they run *him* down where you've been ? " The answer, " Oh, yes, Billy ; they always do it," would delight him, and he would exclaim in joy, " Then he *must* be guilty! He must be! He hasn't got a leg to stand on !"

But he looked upon *him* from a commercial standpoint as well, and said once to a dignitary of St. George's Chapel, " You're always running *him* down.   But he's the best friend you ever 'ad.   If 't 'adn't bin for him, you'd have had nothing to do !"

In the hot weather, one afternoon, two or three years before his death, he became faint in the Chapel, and had to be taken out. One of the Military Knights who dwell in the Castle sent him a glass of port wine, which he took at a gulp.

A lay-clerk said to him in sympathy, " I suppose it was the hot weather ? " " It's 'otter somewhere else—where *he* is !" Billy shouted.

He, according to Billy, was conversant with all that was going on, delighted in setting people by the ears, and, above all other vices, took in the local papers every week !

It is averred by certain people who knew Billy, that in his early days he understood well what were the chief points in the doctrine of Christianity, and what was or was not a good sermon. He could talk with ease of public events, and a preacher who chose a text not according to his ideas of the day met with terribly off-hand censure. Billy Leggett was never able to follow any trade, and in the old days helped his mother by turning her mangle.

Directly, however, the time for the Eton service approached, persuasion was useless, and Billy was off at once. He lived then in Bier Lane, and the Eton and St. George's Chapel services followed each other, so that the choristers at the first could take part in the second. This was in Dean Hobart's time. One of the singing-men was blind and lame, yet could not be excused, and Billy was accustomed to conduct him to Eton and thence back to St. George's.

Now and then, on the return journey, the ring of the Chapel bell was heard ere they reached Windsor, and Billy would be at once furious, let go his charge, and toddle off without mercy. Billy was very fond of Luther's hymn, and prevailed one evening upon Sir George to hear him sing it in the chorister's singing-school. Billy's chief desire was to present well a remarkable shake which one of the then lay-clerks was wont to introduce at the end; and after he had succeeded to his own full satisfaction, he requested further that Sir George would ask the Dean to let him sing the hymn in the Chapel next day as an anthem! saying in an off-hand manner, "If you'll tell him my name is Leggett, he'll know all about me."

He did one day succeed, without limit, in securing for himself a highly distinguished position for the time being. We give his own version of the story. Once a year the choristers belonging to Billy's two places of worship had what they called their Eton feast, and for that afternoon the service at St. George's was omitted. Billy was always an invited guest, and on one of the occasions, in the interval between the beef and the plum-pudding, the St. George's bell began to ring. No one could hold him back, and off he toddled to Windsor.

The Dean and Canons were then obliged to keep twenty-one days' residence in succession, and, either through inadvertence, or (as some say) to secure himself from losing his residence, Dean Hobart had most unexpectedly arranged for service. He read it himself, and his sole auditor was Billy, who likewise made himself responsible for the preces and the chants.

The Dean, wanting apparently to shorten the service, omitted the Magnificat and was going on with the Nunc Dimittis. This was too much for Billy. He rushed to the Dean in his stall, and exclaimed, in more than a whisper, " My soul doth magnify ! " " Oh, ah ! " was the quiet reply, and Dean Hobart went back to the proper place.

The Dean was very kind to Billy's mother, and, when she lay ill, sent her some jam. On her death, Billy went forthwith to the Dean and said, " Please, sir, mother's dead; may I eat the jam ? "

Billy died in January, 1875, and Sir George, who had always taken a kindly interest in the poor eccentric creature, collected funds and had a tombstone erected to his memory in Windsor cemetery, bearing the following inscription :

IN MEMORY OF

WILLIAM LEGGETT,

FOR UPWARDS OF 50 YEARS

A REGULAR ATTENDANT AT THE DAILY SERVICES

OF ST. GEORGE'S CHAPEL.

DIED JAN. 23, 1875,

AGED 73 YEARS.

Lord, I have loved the habitation of Thy house.— *Ps.* xxvi. 8.

The entrance of Thy Word giveth light ; it giveth understanding unto the simple.—*Ps.* cxix. 130.

Wise, the sexton at St. George's during this period, was another oddity, who used to greatly amuse frequenters of the Chapel by his eccentricities and absurd remarks.

He had a great affection for long words and high-sounding phrases, which, however, he could rarely contrive to use in their proper form or place.   He was a thorough Mr. Malaprop.

A clergyman once hurried into the nave of St. George's before service, and remarked that he had walked all the way from Bishopsgate in less than an hour.   To which Wise replied: "Well, you *must* be a good Presbyterian, then!"

One evening, Dr. Bridge and Dr. Keeton, who were then residing in Windsor, took Wise up to London to the Italian opera.

After the performance had begun, one of them said to him, " I fear you don't understand much of this, Wise ? "

They were somewhat astonished when he promptly replied: "Ah! you forget I was three years in France!"

He once remarked of Dean Wellesley, whom he saw taking a constitutional outside the Chapel: " Look at the Dean, a-propagating up and down them steps!"

According to his own account, Wise's favourite paper was the " Ulcerated News."

This man was fully under the impression that the Chapel belonged to him, and that no one had a right to see any part of it without remunerating him. "It doesn't matter," said Wise on one occasion, "it doesn't matter who it is. Nobody —not even Mr. Dean himself—can't go in the Chapel without first *insulting* me!"

He at last carried this to such an extent that he defeated his own object, for the Dean and Canons forbade any further gratuities to be given to the vergers.

CHAPTER XXVIII.

IN the summer of 1875 Sir George lost his eldest son from paralysis, brought on, it was said, by smoking while too young, and also probably by a slight sunstroke whilst boating on the river.

He had been ill for a long time, and this sorrow weighed heavily on his father.

It is wonderful, in considering Sir George's chequered life, to think how his sensitive soul succeeded in rising superior to the many troubles he was called upon to suffer, and in putting self aside in what he felt was his life-work—the promoting of the honour and glory of God in the worship of the sanctuary. His work for this end was unceasing; no private engagements, no private pleasures, were undertaken if they were likely to interfere with this. Rarely, indeed, except for a short three weeks' holiday in the year, was he absent from the Chapel.

Although invariably of a somewhat serious and earnest mood when engaged in his work, he was decidedly cheerful and even playful when free from responsibilities. Mr. Hancock in speaking of this says : " His cheerfulness showed itself very plainly when he was preparing for or enjoying a holiday. I remember once assisting him in packing some luggage when he was leaving home, and, as he put up his razors, he admonished me never to begin shaving if I could help it, as it was such a great bother. 'If you do so at all,' he said, 'you had better begin by practising on the cat!'"

*   *   *   *   *

In June, 1876, Sir George's daughter, Nellie, was bridesmaid to Anna Savory, who married the Rev. J. H. Johnson, Rector of Brocklesby, Lincolnshire, and Sir George kindly went over to Sunningdale and played the service for his old pupil.

Curiously enough, it was on this same day, six years later, that he married Mrs. Johnson's sister.

They had both been kind friends to his children, almost from their babyhood, his youngest son, Charles, being but eighteen months old when the friendship commenced.

In July another of the festivals in aid of the Choir Benevolent Fund took place in St. George's Chapel under his direction.

The festival service was drawn up in a similar

form to that used on previous occasions, except that, of course, variety was made by having a different selection of anthems. The choir, as was usual on any special event, was supplemented by gentlemen and choristers from the Chapel Royal, St. Paul's, Westminster Abbey, and Eton College, and by a small orchestra.

The programme included " Lift up thine eyes !" by Sir John Goss. The veteran composer was by the side of Sir George in the organ-loft, and, as the last strains of his anthem died away, he turned, and with tears in his eyes, and in a voice broken by deep feeling, exclaimed, "Ah ! I never hear my anthems done as they are here."

In December there was a grand performance at the Castle, when Sir George played the organ.

Miss Sophie Ferrari, Miss Jessie Jones, and Madame Trebelli were the soloists, and selections were given from " Athalie." Amongst other items a cantique, " Noel," was sung by Mr. Cummings and the chorus. A month later the Windsor and Eton Madrigal Society gave a performance before the Queen in St. George's Hall, Windsor Castle. At this, Sir George's motet, " Hark ! those voices," was sung. It is written for two choirs, and when the distant one, which was concealed, commenced, it created not a little surprise and interest among the audience present.

At the close of the concert, the Queen spoke most kindly to Sir George, and said how much she had enjoyed the evening. H.R.H. Princess Christian very kindly wrote to him afterwards, saying she was sure he would like to know how pleased the Queen was with the singing, how highly she approved the programme, and especially admired Sir George's own two compositions, " The Zetland Fishermen," and " Hark! those voices."

Soon after this, he wrote his piano gavotte, " A la mode ancienne," curiously enough, for a concert at Windlesham, Surrey, in which village he spent the last years of his life.

Sir George at this time interested himself much in trying to draw the attention of the Deans and Chapters to the growing deterioration in the style of music introduced into the cathedrals. He often used to say of the old Church composers that "they did not give unto God that which cost them nothing;" they spared neither time nor brains to produce the finest music of which they were capable; and he mourned, with many friends, that these magnificent and devotional works should be cast on one side, in many cathedrals, for those of a light, secular style resembling the masses used in Roman Catholic churches. In 1877 he drew up the following letter to the Deans and Canons upon the subject :

"The Cloisters, Windsor.

" REVEREND GENTLEMEN,

"You will, I hope, forgive the liberty I am taking in venturing to call your attention to the present sad state of things as regards Church music in our cathedrals. I do so, in the hope that I may be able to stem the torrent of bad taste, which is rapidly destroying our ancient and glorious style of Church music, and substituting for it services and anthems which have little to recommend them but novelty. I would plead that when so much pains is being taken by all, especially the clergy, to have our fine old cathedrals restored to their original beauty, under the care of that eminent and conservative architect, Sir Gilbert Scott, and others, the music performed in them should be in keeping with the grandeur of the edifice, and should remind all who hear that they are in a sacred building. Now, the good old Church music does this, and I feel it a duty to raise my voice to try and rescue the grand compositions of our great English Church composers from falling into oblivion and neglect; for, although my efforts may fail, I shall have the satisfaction of knowing that I have called the attention to this subject of those who have the power to remedy the evil. It would be unbecoming in me to say one word respecting modern Church composers, but I am quite satisfied we have men who would write good Church music, provided there was any appreciation of their efforts.

" I am, reverend gentlemen,

" Your obedient servant,

(Signed) " G. J. ELVEY."

To this letter the following was added :

" We, the undersigned, do cordially agree to the above, and are glad to co-operate with Sir George Elvey in his praiseworthy efforts to improve the present prospects of English Cathedral music.

" FREDERICK G. OUSELEY, BART.

" ARTHUR SULLIVAN.

" C. W. CORFE.

" JAMES TURLE.

" J. HOPKINS.

" G. A. MACFARREN.

" EDWIN GEORGE MONK."

The feelings of these eminent musicians on the solemnity that there ought to be in Church music seem to have been shared by Mendelssohn (whom Sir George greatly admired), for he wrote thus :

" I have found, to my astonishment, that the Catholics, who have had music in their churches for several centuries, and sing a musical mass every Sunday, if possible, in their principal churches, do not, to this day, possess one which can be considered even tolerably good, or, in fact, which is not actually distasteful and operatic. This is the case from Pergolese and Durante, who introduce the most laughable little trills into their Glorias, down to the opera finales of the present day.

" Were I a Catholic, I would set to work at a mass this very evening, and, whatever it might turn out, it would, at all events, be the only mass written with a constant remembrance of its sacred purpose ! "

In connection with the letter to the Deans, etc., Sir George wrote the following to a friend :

" Windsor,
" March 20th, 1877.

" MY DEAR . . . .

" I was induced to write my letter on the present state of Church music by hearing of several cathedrals where Gibbons in F was *un-known !* Surely this is enough to move the wrath of anyone who venerates what is good in ecclesiastical music. As far as my own judgment goes, I think the day is not far distant when Boyce's three volumes will become ' a sealed book and a dead letter.'

" I am glad that in your cathedral the old masters are fully represented; it is not so in *many*. I by no means wish to exclude modern music; very much of late years has been written which I always play at St. George's with great pleasure. I am pressed, as you doubtless are, to play many things contrary to my taste and judgment, but even this I do not rebel against, so long as the REAL good style is not *utterly neglected. . . . Good* modern services are few and far between."

Sir George was much delighted with a speech made a few years before by Dr. Arnold of Winchester, respecting the great deterioration of modern hymn-tunes at the Church Congress at Bath, and he wrote thus at the time :

" I quite agree with you about modern hymn-tunes; they, in many instances, resemble German part-songs, a very poor style of vocal writing at

the best, and a very long way behind our good
old English glees.   I consider your protest a very
courageous one, and I hope it will produce a good
effect; but those who are bold enough to tell the
truth must, I expect, be prepared for a little rough
treatment; but never mind this, you have with
you the sympathy and support of all right-minded
people, and especially of,

"Yours very truly,

(Signed) " G. J. Elvey."

Mr. Curwen says :

" I feel that the conservative element in English
musical feeling is of great value.   It prevents us
catching the craze of the hour, and drifting here,
there, and everywhere; and the influence of men
like Sir George Elvey, exerted through his
choristers and pupils, is of immense value in
maintaining the solidity and caution of our
musical judgments."

CHAPTER XXIX.

THE summer and autumn of 1878 were a very sad time. First, in June, came the funeral of the King of Hanover, and later in the year the death of H.R.H. Princess Alice, on December 14th. On the 18th Sir George played at the memorial service held in the private chapel on the day of her funeral.

For this he wrote " The Souls of the Righteous " —that lovely, solemn, and touching anthem which has since been performed at his own funeral, which took place on the anniversary of Princess Alice's death.

During the greater part of this year Sir George's wife had been ailing, and in the summer he went with her for a few weeks to Harrogate, hoping that the waters there would restore her to health. Unfortunately, however, the change did not effect the good that was anticipated, and week by week, and month by month, the terrible illness increased

which culminated in her death early in January of
1879.

She bore her suffering with much fortitude, but
it was a great trial for those who loved her to
witness the fearful agony she often endured.

The March following her death saw another
royal ceremonial in Windsor—of a very different
character to the last, for now everything was full
of brightness and life—in preparation for the
marriage of the Duke of Connaught to the
Princess Louise Margaret of Prussia.

So strangely do joy and sorrow intermingle
in this life !

The wedding was a very brilliant scene, and
the arrangements were carried out with almost, or
quite, as much splendour as those for the marriage
of the Prince of Wales had been.

The scene in the Chapel was a magnificent one ;
the scarlet coats of the officers and military
knights lining either side of the carpet from the
screen to the altar-rails ; the splendid court
dresses of the ladies glistening with diamonds ;
all combined to form a picture to which the noble
architecture of the glorious old Chapel was a fitting
framework.

Again Sir George had to rouse himself from his

own sorrows to prepare and arrange the music for this grand occasion.

So thoroughly successful were his untiring exertions, and so satisfied was the Queen with the result, that she sent him a very handsome cup as a memento.

During the summer he spent some weeks in Scotland, staying not far from Edinburgh, and making various pleasant excursions in the neighbourhood.

On his way back he visited Mr. and Mrs. Johnson, at Brocklesby Rectory, and opened their new organ, which had been built under his direction. Here he was ever an eagerly-welcomed guest. Mrs. Johnson was an old pupil of his, and she and her husband both greatly admired and esteemed his beautiful Christian character.

Later still, he went for a few days to visit once again the scenes of his childhood at Canterbury. This was a painful pleasure, for all the friends that he knew there in his early days, except Dr. Long hurst, the present organist, had passed away.

This summer Sir George had rather a longer holiday, as the Chapel was closed for cleaning.

But work, hard and unceasing, is always the best remedy for sorrow, and he really felt it a relief when the Chapel was re-opened, and he was back again at his post.

He loved his organ, and he loved the Chapel, having watched it gradually emerge from the whitewash and destruction of Cromwell, under skilful hands, to its former stately grandeur. Truly,

> "A noble fane . . . .
> A regal temple, where to worship Him,
> Before Whom all the kings of earth bow down."

How different now to when he, as Mr. Elvey, was first introduced to it, few, indeed, remain to tell! Hard it is to realize that the beauties of "fretted roof," and walls and pillars "enriched with sculptured work and tracery of gold," were veiled from sight by a thick covering of lime and dust. Even the oak stalls were so encrusted with varnish and dirt, that the exquisite carving was almost hidden from view; and it was a work of no little patience and trouble to cleanse and restore them to their present condition.

The dangerous state in which the stonework of the west window had been for a long time, and the great probability that the whole of the mullions, and very likely part of the gable above might suddenly fall, induced the Chapter, in October, 1842, to rebuild it, preserving accurately all its original form and dimension.

The glass occupying the openings was of the time of King Henry VII., and consisted partly of fifty-nine figures of saints, prophets, kings, and knights, all of which had been removed to this window from various parts of the Chapel in 1774, by Dr. Lockman, who had placed the figures on a ground of clear white glass.

The remaining openings were filled by reticulated patterns in common and glaring colours, placed also on clear glass.

After the restoration of the stonework the plain ground of white glass was removed and superseded by ancient diaper patterns in a quiet tone of drab. Ten more of the ancient figures still remained in the stalls of the Chapter; with these, and by the addition of six new effigies, the glaziers' patterns were excluded, and every opening was occupied by a whole-length figure.

Rich canopies, columns, and bases were added to them, and on a scroll which now runs through the whole of the bases of the lowest compartments, is inscribed the prayer, peculiar to the service at St. George's:

" God save our Gracious Sovereign, and all the

companions of the Most Honourable and Noble Order of the Garter."

This window was always an immense pleasure to Sir George, who had seen its restoration. Day after day he would, in the afternoon, watch from the organ-loft, with intense delight, its exquisite appearance when lit up by the setting sun.

For some time after he went to Windsor, two old helmets were lying about in the Dean's garden quite uncared-for and unthought-of, until one morning a man came down from London to see the Dean about his account for work done for the Chapter. This account was considered too heavy, but the man was very unwilling to reduce it, until suddenly remembering the helmets he had spied outside, he said : " Well, Mr. Dean, if you will give me those two helmets, I will accept the sum you propose." Quite pleased to be rid of these encumbrances from his garden, the man's account was promptly settled by the Dean on these terms, and the helmets ere long were transferred to their new home in the window of an old curiosity shop in London.

But they were not to rest there long, for the Garter King-at-Arms, having spied these trophies, made anxious inquiries from whence they had come, and when the story of their origin was unfolded, he went in a towering rage to Windsor, and ordered the Dean and Canons to bring them back.

The railway not then being open, a carriage and four was at once procured, and in this one of the Canons immediately drove to London, and in due time returned with the spoils, which were promptly returned to the Chapel, from whence they had originally been abstracted, but not even then were they placed in their legitimate places.

Some years after, during the restoration of the Chapel, these poor helmets were again turned out, and were this time thrown into the Crypt. From thence they were once more rescued, this time by Dr. Elvey, who with much trouble discovered at last to whom they belonged; by his efforts they were placed near the tombs of the kings whose heads they had adorned.

Not many days before his death, when talking of St. George's, he said that he believed it was at his suggestion that the Knights of the Garter had been asked to subscribe to refill the niches outside with figures, which was the last important restoration executed.

For years he had wished to have a good music-room in Windsor, as the Town Hall was such an unsatisfactory place for concerts, and St. Mark's School, which, by the kindness of the Rev. Stephen Hawtrey, had been for the last few years lent for concerts, was not always available.

Therefore it was with no little pleasure that he welcomed the completion of the Albert Institute, and in April, 1880, gladly again lent his aid in arranging the music for the opening ceremony, which was performed by H.R.H. the Prince of Wales. For it he specially composed " Let us now praise famous men," scored for a full band.

Some months later he went down to Brighton to act as umpire at a military band competition held in the Pavilion. The last important event in which he took part, just before he left Windsor, was the marriage of the Duke of Albany to Princess Helen of Waldeck, which took place at St. George's Chapel on May 6th, 1882. The arrangements of the musical portion of this service, under his direction, gave such satisfaction to H.M. the Queen that she presented him with a very handsome silver claret jug.

Thus practically closed the public life of one of

the greatest geniuses of the present century, a man
"who has left his mark on English cathedral
music," and withal one of the most modest and
simple-minded men that ever lived.

He was rarely free from an active interest
in some one or other, who, through misfor-
tunes of various kinds, had been unsuccessful in
the battle of life, and he took a genuine pleasure,
being singularly free from jealousy of any kind, in
lending a helping hand that other members of his
profession might climb a rung higher on the ladder
to fame, although this would often put him to a
great deal of trouble and even personal inconvenience.

That there are some who are free to admit their
obligations to him, the following extracts from
letters will show :

" I have been told to-day, that you lost your dear
husband, and I my dear master, benefactor, and
friend, yesterday. . . . Many will call his name
blessed, and revere his memory. . . . If I am
mentioned in your book, I should wish my immense
obligations to Sir George to be stated in the most
emphatic manner. I believe that only in the next
world will all his good works come to light. He
was one who did not let his left hand know the

good his right hand did. 'His works do follow him.'

"Yours truly,

"E. H. THORNE."

*　　*　　*　　*　　*

"Such of his pupils as knew him best must all share your grief, in the knowledge that they have lost a friend whose place in their affection no one else can fill. . . . He was not only my master, but during all the years I was with him, as chorister, articled pupil, or assistant, he took a father's interest in my welfare, nor has his kindness diminished to this day. . .

"CHARLES HANCOCK."

*　　*　　*　　*　　*

"I have lost a friend *indeed*, for he has been a father to me, one who always sympathized with me in all my troubles and difficulties, and was ever ready to give advice in time of need.

"His death has caused a void that can never be refilled. . . .

"What he did for me in that terrible calamity that befell me some years ago, you very well know. Had it not been for his encouraging letters and God's providence, I should surely have been crushed and ruined, not only temporally, but eternally.

"When I look back through the past years, I can see him again—a man whose sole aim in life was to do his duty, however disagreeable, in his calling, and as far as in him lay, to live peaceably with all men. His Christian belief was 'deeds,' and many were they that no one knew but himself, for he rarely let his right hand know what his left hand did. And now let us look at him in his resting-place. Yes, after a busy and active life, of the trials and troubles of which (speaking reverently) he had his share, he is now at rest, and gone to learn that heavenly song, the earthly part of which he spent so many years in cultivating; and has left us to mourn, not for him, but the great vacancy he has left in that circle of true friends which, as we grow older, appears to contract so rapidly.

"I . . . add my mite of admiration of his noble character, and a last tribute of esteem and love for my never-to-be-forgotten dearest friend and master.

"GEORGE PEARSON."

*   *   *   *   *

The Rev. J. R. Matthews thus writes of him after his death :

" His was a character for which everyone must

feel the greatest admiration—no vanity or egotism, no insincerity, no humbug of any kind, but a real straight, honest, manly John Bull.

"On his resigning his position at St. George's I wrote to him, and suggested to him the thought of the many souls who for ages to come will pour forth their praises, and send up their prayers to God, in the beautiful strains he was inspired to compose. That he now rests in peace who can doubt? May I be permitted to share his happy lot!"

CHAPTER XXX.

SIR GEORGE had been a widower for about three and a half years. He felt his loneliness so keenly, being naturally dependent upon companionship and sympathy, that it seriously affected his health ; and the continual strain incidental to his position—acting on a temperament highly-strung and sensitive in the extreme—made his friends fearful for his life, and many of them predicted that he would not live two years.

However, acting on good advice, he summoned up courage to try and win for himself his old pupil and friend, Miss Mary Savory, of Buckhurst Park, with the result that on June 20th he was most happily united to one with whom he spent eleven and a half years of almost perfect happiness, only marred by external worries over which he had no control. He then retired from his post at Windsor, and his reasons for resigning are well known to those who created them, and must, or at least should, fill them with lifelong pain and remorse. Never did a man more entirely throw his whole life and energy into his work, or more conscientiously strive, not only to do his duty, but without grudge or stint to serve everyone around him, and words fail to express the cruel treatment and base ingratitude of which he was the victim.

. Such was the reward of a life's faithful service ! This must ever be a blot on the annals of Windsor. But his heart was surely fixed on the Rock of Ages, and he felt that it is enough for the servant that he be as his Master, who endured " such contradiction of sinners against himself," and he sought and found grace from above to bear, in the most saintly manner, his bitter trials. Not a murmur, not one unkind word he permitted to escape his lips.

Occasionally, while thinking of the past, in his now happy home, he would give a sigh of sadness when he thought of those who, ever ready to accept his help in endless ways, now, when he was no longer able to exert himself so much, had forgotten their old friend. It would flash across his mind how true the proverb, " Out of sight, out of mind," but it was only a passing shadow, for he loved better to dwell on how wonderfully and

AT THE ORGAN
A WINDSOR

mercifully God had watched over and dealt with him all his life.

That his upright and consistent conduct, and his earnest, persevering work during his long tenure of office were generally appreciated, will be seen by the following passages, taken from various sources after his death :

"The death of Sir George Elvey on Saturday morning removes from the musical profession a talented organist, a fluent writer of refined compositions of an ecclesiastical character, a kind teacher, and a thorough gentleman.

"Numerous anthems and hymn-tunes were the products of his pen, by which his name will long live in the annals of Church music.

*   *   *   *   *

"Sir George personally was a most charming man, without a shadow of self-assertion, and yet full of spirit and anecdote. He was an excellent trainer of choirs, and understood the development of boys' voices more thoroughly than any of his contemporaries. . . . He was intolerant of slovenly performances, and untiring in his efforts to promote efficiency. His occupancy of the post of organist to the Chapel Royal was a memorable one.

*   *   *   *   *

" He was a very fine organ-player, and his name will live through his beautiful anthems, which are constantly sung in every cathedral in England.

" The music and singing at St. George's were always excellent during his long term of office.

*　　*　　*　　*　　*

" Sir George Elvey, who has done such masterly work for Church music amongst us, leaving his name upon the cathedral music of the time, died on Saturday last.　He was a masterly organ-player, and may be said to have founded a school of organ-playing of his own.

" He was appointed organist of St. George's Chapel in 1835, and two years afterwards became organist to the Queen.　He was a great favourite with the royal family, particularly with Prince Albert, and was a frequent guest at both Osborne and Windsor.

*　　*　　*　　*　　*

" He was a musician, noted for his reticence and modesty, no less than his solid gifts.

*　　*　　*　　*　　*

" As as accompanist on the organ he was without a rival."

*　　*　　*　　*　　*

A gentleman now residing in Windsor speaks

thus of the impression made upon him many years ago by Sir George's organ-playing :

" Having heard of his fame I took the opportunity of attending the service at St. George's Chapel on the afternoon of September 10th, 1847.[1] I am never likely to forget the impression made by Dr. Elvey in his accompaniment of the 78th Psalm. The organ upon which he then played was a considerably smaller affair than the experts amongst organists of the present day will put up with. Nevertheless, the effects produced in that truly dramatic Psalm I have never heard equalled, nor do I think I am now likely again to hear it.

" As a Londoner I took every opportunity of visiting Windsor with my family in holiday seasons, and eventually I settled down as a Windsor resident in 1883, for the purpose of enjoying a service that for thirty-six years I had never failed to extol amongst friends, clerical and musical, as the best in all England. I was by no means happy at finding the bird of harmony had flown !

---

[1] " I shall never forget the date," said he, and named it instantly, without reference to any note, and without being fore-warned that the subject might be introduced.

"On many occasions, when at Windsor, I had been tempted to seek an introduction to Sir George, and might easily have obtained one through friends, but I esteemed him too much to encroach upon that dignified demeanour which became him so well, without giving the least suspicion of arrogance.

"To the last I have been gratified at witnessing the annual ovation accorded him by his old friends at Windsor at the yearly concert given by the gentlemen of the St. George's Chapel choir. I little thought on October 26th, 1893, that I then saw him for the last time."

Mr. Robert Lyttleton says : "Sir George in his accompanying of the Psalms has never to my mind been surpassed, and no one has excelled him as a chant composer."

CHAPTER XXXI.

RENEWED happiness, combined with the fine air of South Ascot, where he had taken a house, soon restored him to better health than he had enjoyed for very many years, and with the return of this, and the cessation from the work and excitement of his profession, the nervousness and depression from which he had suffered so much to a great extent disappeared.

This was much noticed by his friends, and one of his former pupils who came to see him writes thus:

"It is very gratifying to know that with the cessation of professional responsibilities he has to a great extent lost his excessive nervousness, and now enjoys a peaceful and happy life in comfortable retirement."

Although at one time he had fully made up his mind that if his life were spared he should like to celebrate his jubilee at St. George's before retiring, yet the relief of being perfectly free after so many years of trammel was such that he was never heard to lament the step he had taken in resigning his post.

When he first contemplated leaving Windsor he feared that time would hang heavily on his hands, but this was in reality never the case, for he revelled in the country, and day by day, careless of weather, might be seen in the grounds surrounding his house superintending various operations connected with laying out the garden—draining, etc. When tired of this he would amuse himself by revising his music, looking over various pieces sent to him by friends eager for his assistance (which his kindly heart never permitted him to refuse). Thus, we find him writing to a young friend:

"I have looked over your music. . . . The anthem is too short, and in future attempts avoid the D. C.; if a part is to be repeated, let it be done with some change of harmony, etc. See Mendelssohn's melody in the fourth book of the 'Lieder.' Have you studied fugue? If you have, when you write another anthem or organ-piece give some proof of it. I will at all times look over anything you send me, and pray *do not be dis-*

couraged; you can and will, I have no doubt, send me something better next time."

As the examinations came round at the various colleges, he would busy himself with the examination papers.

Later in the day he would drive to Buckhurst, the home of Lady Elvey's mother, where, with her, he spent many happy hours each week cheering Mrs. Savory in her widowhood. She was very fond of him, and used to say she had never met anyone with such a guileless childlike spirit. She greatly enjoyed a chat with him concerning the many scenes and stately ceremonials he had witnessed in Windsor, but often the conversation would glide to higher themes, connected with eternity, on which both loved to dwell.

Another great delight to her, was to induce him to play to her, for Sir George's piano-playing was, as has been said of his accompanying, "A thing to hear and not forget." His touch was simply exquisite, and in his hands the instrument truly spoke.

Frequently would he sit down, at the urgent request of his friends, and enchant his hearers with his rendering of some of Mendelssohn's Lieder, selections from Beethoven or Corelli, or a succession of national airs arranged and woven together as he alone could do it.

He was also a very fine violin-player, and used to play with Lady Elvey all Beethoven's sonatas; most, if not all, of Mozart; in fact, nearly all the duets that they could procure for violin and piano. He was very fond of playing quartettes, and on one of these occasions Mr. Henry Blagrove expressed his great admiration of his playing, while Mr. J. S. Liddle, another accomplished violinist, writes of it as follows:

"Though I had often seen Sir George before, the first time I was introduced to him was in 1872, at a quartette meeting held at the house of the Rev. W. H. Bliss in the Cloisters. The parts of the Beethoven Op. 18, No. 1, were given me for distribution, and I naturally handed Sir George the first fiddle. He played through the first movement in excellent style, apparently without noticing what his part was. But at the end of it he turned to me saying, 'Come, young gentleman, none of your tricks on travellers; hand me up that second fiddle part.'

"Few know how very good a player he really was. The main public use to which he put his playing, was in alternately conducting and leading, from the conductor's desk, at the Windsor Choral Society's concerts, a method which entailed a somewhat rough-and-ready style. But in a room, where I have more than once had the honour of accompanying him, his style was most refined, and his intonation of a fascinating degree of delicacy rarely heard in these days of all-prevailing equal temperament.

" The study of the violin was part of the course he gave all his articled pupils, one of whom I was lucky enough to become, although, as a rule, he only took boys from his own choir. He gave no regular lessons to us, but we could always have one by asking for it, and I still feel with gratitude the fruits of his sound and careful instruction in pianoforte-playing. He was extremely particular about the position of the hands, and most scrupulous as regards systematic fingering. It was probably this which gave his own playing its spotless correctness. One listened to him twice a day on the organ, sometimes for many weeks, without hearing a suspicion of a wrong note."

The one sport to which Sir George had always lent himself, when his professional engagements would admit, was an afternoon or evening spent in fishing, and many were the visits made, during the summer, with one of his friends or pupils, to Black Pots, Staines, Egham, Datchet, and Shepperton, from which places he generally returned well laden with spoil.

While following this favourite pastime as a boy, he once narrowly escaped being drowned. He had been fishing from a wall by the riverside, but not being very successful, he climbed down on to some scaffold-boards by the side of the water. One of these, being insecurely fixed, gave a sudden jerk, and the ill-fated young fisherman was precipitated head foremost into the river, being subsequently rescued in a drowning condition.

Sometimes, while at Buckhurst, in later years, when mother and daughter, who were wrapped up in one another, were chatting happily together, Sir George would wander down to the lake with his rod, and enjoy an hour's fishing, a pastime for which he never lost his affection.

On one occasion, fishing in a friend's lake, he caught a fine jack, which he safely landed, and, resuming his sport, congratulated himself on the prize he had secured.

Looking round shortly afterwards, he observed a pig quietly demolishing the spoil !

On another expedition he caught a pike which

scaled nearly ten pounds. Of this fine specimen
he was very proud, and it now reposes, stuffed, in
a glass case in the hall at Windlesham.

During the summer of 1882 Sir George and
his wife went to Scarborough, and thence to
Brocklesby, the home of Lady Elvey's favourite
sister—a trip that Sir George always alluded to
as a most enjoyable one. His visits to Brocklesby,
throughout these later years, were among his
greatest pleasures. He much enjoyed the society
of his brother-in-law, and he would frequently
wander down to the little clematis-covered cottage
at the end of the drive, where Mr. Johnson's father
lived in retirement, and patiently help the old man
of ninety-two to master the difficulties of a
harmonium, the great solace of his blindness.

It was always a pleasure to him to aid anyone
who needed assistance, and visitors to his home in
later years love to recall the kind offers to hear
them play, and the patience shown, and encouragement ungrudgingly given, when their performances
must have tortured his keenly-sensitive ear.

On Sundays, during his visits to Brocklesby, he
always played the service in the pretty little
church, to the great delight of the villagers; and
he would give hints and assist in the training of

the choir. The men and boys composing it were an endless source of amusement to him. Often he would laugh at the recollection, as memory painted him their picture: standing at attention, with words grasped in one hand, and music in the other.

The paper must needs have exerted some magic spell, for none among them could read a note. One, in particular, he always inquired for as " my ancient friend." This man's qualifications for his post were undiscovered—he certainly did not possess the slightest ear for music.

(In after years the choir greatly improved, and Sir George used frequently to express his approbation of their work. Indeed, the last time he was there, in June, 1893, he was delighted at the progress they had made, and especially admired the chanting of the Psalms, which they did most intelligently from his brother's Psalter. He specially wrote an anthem for this choir to sing at a harvest festival.)

The long drives in the beautiful park surrounding Brocklesby Hall, Lord Yarborough's country home, added much to the enjoyment of these visits. Many pleasant afternoons were spent in this way, Lady Elvey driving her husband in a little carriage drawn by an old grey pony, which animal had a decided will of his own, and one method alone was successful in inducing him to proceed beyond a walk, viz., shouting at him!

Sir George evidently retained a vivid recollection of his efforts in this direction, for he wrote, later on, in fun, for Lady Elvey, a round to the words, "Gee-up, Dobbin, gee-up and gee-whoa!"

Soon after his return from Lincolnshire he was invited by Sir Joseph Savory to the sheriffs' banquet, and, as winter drew on, he set to work to prepare a part-song in honour of Lord Wolseley's return from Egypt—the words being supplied by Lady Elvey.

At the latter end of the autumn, Mr. (now Sir Walter) Parratt, his successor at St. George's, begged him to come over and play the farewell services on his "dear old organ" before it was altered. This he did, and gave for the last time his splendid rendering of his brother's Service in A, and Boyce's anthem, "Oh, where shall wisdom be found?"

Not long after he left Windsor, he prepared, at Mr. Parratt's request, chants for a month's services, with a chant arranged for every psalm. This was a work involving no little labour, and he bestowed almost endless time and attention on it; it was the third month of chants that he had arranged, two having been prepared for his own use at St. George's.

The first month's were special favourites, and not long since, among other applications for a copy, Sir George received one from Copenhagen.

In June, 1883, a little son was born to him, who later on was christened by the names George Frederic Handel.

Always fond of children, and possessing in an unusual degree the power of attracting them to him, and sympathizing with and amusing them, it was a great delight to him to have a child once more about the house; and " the little chap," as he always called him, grew up with a reverence for, and devotion to his father seldom equalled.

Just at this time Sir George was presented with his portrait, which had been painted by Mr. Val Prinsep, R.A., at a concert of the Windsor and Eton Madrigal Society, the presentation being made by H.R.H. Princess Christian.

When the picture came home, Handel, though only five months old, regarded it with intense interest and no little astonishment, gazing first at his father, and then at the portrait. Sir George often alluded to the circumstance with great amusement.

The following extracts from letters will show the delight he took in his little son :

" Baby is well, and very good and happy ; his little tongue goes on from morning till night, and he has a way now of hanging upon his last word, which has a very comical effect. He called my attention to a cow, drinking wate—r in Bristow's picture in the dining-room. I had a rare game of romps with him this morning in his bed. I am glad to hear your dear mother is better, so I shall hope to find her pretty well when I come (D.V.) to-morrow."

*   *   *   *   *

" I went in the brougham yesterday, and took Baby with me. I had him alone, and he was very good indeed. I called upon Mrs. ——. Baby went into the house with me, and behaved himself like a gentleman. Mr. —— showed him some things, with which he was much amused, particularly with a lady riding on a donkey, and he enlightened all present with his explanations of it. He is very happy, and talks incessantly. He sat on my knee last evening, and explained all the pictures in the little fat book you had with him on Monday evening."

At this time Handel was not quite two years of age.

As he grew older it was an increasing pleasure to his father to have him with him for a walk or drive, and it was a pretty sight to see the two together. When, on the rare occasions that Lady Elvey was away for several hours, she would ask the child to look after Sir George during her absence, Handel would fulfil his mission to the letter.

Leaving soldiers, bricks, and toys, of which he had a thorough child's love, he would spend hours together, sitting opposite his father, trying to talk on subjects that he thought would amuse and please him.

The big eyes would grow wide with interest, and the forehead pucker with endeavours to understand, as his father, forgetful for a moment in the earnestness of his listener, of the little child who was his companion, would launch forth into some pet topic concerning politics, music, or whatever might be uppermost in his mind.

His little son's patience never failed, though sometimes a deep sigh or a rather sleepy, "Yes, Dadda," unconsciously showed his weariness.

CHAPTER XXXII.

NOT long after Sir George took up his residence at La Tour, South Ascot, ever anxious to serve his Master, he willingly offered help in training the choir and playing the services at a little iron mission church, newly erected, a few minutes' walk below his house, in a district of Ascot called the Bog.

The place was a wild one, originally the home of highwaymen, who, in the old days, plied a thriving trade on the main road between London and Exeter. By degrees they settled down, and became to some extent civilized.

Traces of their wild origin still lingered, however, in the younger generation, and the choir-boys proved rough and untameable in the extreme, needing all the patience and kindliness of Sir George to reduce them to some form of order.

On one occasion, at least, these turbulent spirits ranged themselves beside the roadway, and with a volley of stones saluted their teacher on his way home.   Another time, a lad lifted up his hand to strike him, all the latent passion roused by a reproof which one had only to know Sir George to be sure must have been richly merited, and even then gently and patiently given.

When it became known that he was going to undertake the music at the Bog Church several men appeared, expressing a wish to join the choir.

After the work for Sunday had been practised, as was usual, on that night, Sir George, having dismissed the boys, said he should like to try the men's voices.   He tried them one by one with the scale.   The first began with such vigour that Sir George nearly jumped off the stool, exclaiming with surprise, " My conscience, what a shot out of a shovel ! "

For these services he wrote three easy anthems ; one for Easter, " If we believe that Jesus died ; " and two others, unpublished.   Of these, one is, " O praise God in His holiness," and the other, for Christmas, " While shepherds watched their flocks by night."   In preparing the choir with these he spared neither pains nor trouble in order to make the performance as perfect as the somewhat raw material at his disposal admitted of.

In the early years of the church's existence, a harmonium led the services, and Sir George would call attention in a would-be mournful tone to what he had come to !

Worse still, in damp weather (as the little room stood low, with a steep hillock on one side, a state of dampness was not infrequent) the harmonium has been known to fail, but Sir George, not to be daunted by adverse circumstances, would send home for his violin, and the hymns would go with their accustomed vigour. The harmonium was subsequently replaced by an organ, presented by Sir George.

It was a grand sight to see the silver-haired veteran, the first organist of his day, after years of service in one of the noblest churches of our land, for love of the Master whom he served, conducting a service, and filling a post many would have scorned to occupy.

Twice on Sunday, in sunshine or rain, heat or cold, he never missed going to the little church to fulfil his labour of love, and many years he regularly attended the week-night choir practice. His pupil, Mr. E. H. Thorne, writes thus of the simple and touching little service : " I was much struck, a year or two since, when hearing him accompany a service in an iron church at Ascot, by the appropriateness of his accompaniments to the hymns, and by a charm in his playing peculiarly his own. Each hymn had its own proper tempo and expression."

One of his old boys from St. George's, William Amess, was ever very active in assisting him with the choir, and since Sir George's age prevented his attendance at the little church he has filled the place of his beloved master.

For several years Lady Elvey carried on a Band of Hope for the Bog children. In this Sir George took considerable interest, writing new tunes when those in the Services of Song proved too difficult, and himself coming down to assist in teaching the children.

At one of their little concerts a girl of about sixteen was to sing " Jock o' Hazeldean," and Sir George was kindly rehearsing it with her.

This being one of her earliest attempts at solo-singing, she was naturally somewhat nervous at performing before so great a musician, and did not do the song or herself justice, for Sir George remarked, with his usual amusing manner, "Come! let us have it a little better than that ; it is like a yard of pump water."

This roused her to more energy, and taking care to profit by his instruction, she felt well rewarded for the momentary mortification his remark had caused, by the ready approval he accorded her on the evening of the performance.

CHAPTER XXXIII.

AFTER his retirement from Windsor it was his custom to gather round him once a year the gentlemen of the St. George's choir.

This was to him quite a red-letter day, for they all united in efforts to give him pleasure, by preparing to perform as much old and favourite music as a long evening would admit of. None who saw him on these occasions can ever forget the radiant expression on his face as he sat at his dining-table, entertaining his guests with stories from an apparently exhaustless fund, and endeavouring to set both old and new-comers completely at their ease, and, without a thought for himself, straining every nerve to make the evening an enjoyable one to all.

The crowning pleasure, after dinner, before lighter music commenced, was to hear the grand strains of " Non nobis Domine," an old grace by Byrde, composed about 1590. On this piece Sir George counted for days beforehand; and once, when Mr. Hunt asked him if they should sing it, he replied quickly, " Oh ! yes, by all means ; I was singing it all day yesterday in anticipation."

Sir George was a most kind-hearted hospitable man, and none ever entered his doors without a welcome. Although so nervous and retiring in public as sometimes to unfavourably impress casual observers, yet in his own home his genial nature had free play, and he shone greatly as one of the brightest of hosts. He had plenty of anecdote and dry humour for those who were admitted into close relations with him ; and when visitors were staying in the house he would frequently keep his guests in fits of laughter.

Sometimes he would imitate street cries, one of his favourites being that of a woman at Canterbury who sold watercresses.

He described her as carrying a very heavy basket, and singing the following melody :

accompanying the last note with a sudden drop of her burden.

Another was that of a baker's man at Oxford :

Of this man's voice Dr. Stephen Elvey had a very high opinion, and used to say that with proper training he would have made a Braham.

A story Sir George took keen delight in relating was of a Fellow of Magdalen, Oxford, a very nervous man, who never got up if the wind was in the east.

This weakness was speedily found out by the undergraduates, who were not slow to take advantage of it; so, intent on giving him a longer repose than usual, they, by some means, secured the vane in the east, so that he remained in bed until he became suspicious, and found out the trick.

One more tale of this unfortunate gentleman was the following: A lump of butter was placed on his wig by these same mischievous spirits at dinner-time, which, as the room grew warmer, gradually melted and trickling down his face, caused him to turn pale with fright. He at once had a nurse sent for, and retired to bed.

The nurse took up her post beside him, but finding that he soon dropped into a peaceful slumber which seemed likely to continue for some

time, she fell to nodding herself.   After a while
the patient awoke, and promptly aroused his attendant with the cry, uttered in a voice of thunder :

"Why are you asleep? don't you know I am
expecting to die every moment ? "

Another favourite anecdote referred to a very
special occasion in a remote country village, when
an anthem was to be performed by the choir.

After it had been given out, there was an un-
accountably long pause, and at length the old clerk
in despair walked across to the gallery where the
singers were placed, and asked, in anxious tones,
and in something more than a whisper, " Coom,
chaps, bean't ye goin' to sing the ant'em ? "

In a moment the reply came, audibly enough,
" Gettin' the bukes, gettin' the bukes."

Another story of Sir George's refers to an annual
treat which a gentleman at Windsor was in the
habit of giving to the stablemen of George III. at
Christmas time.   On these occasions he always
regaled them with elder wine and biscuits.   Upon
one of these memorable evenings, when they had
been enjoying themselves for some time, he went
to see how they were progressing, and inquired
how they liked the wine.   The man addressed
answered, in broken English (they were mostly

Hanoverians), "Verra much, sir; but 'tis rader too strong of de spice."

"Oh! is it," said the gentleman, "we'll try another bottle."

So saying, he placed a fresh supply upon the table and left the room, but returned ere long and inquired if the wine was better.

"'Tis verra gude, sir; but rader too strong of de spice."

" How very odd," replied the host, at the same time pouring out a sip and raising it to his lips.

Then he exclaimed, with a look of infinite disgust, as he put the glass down again :

" Why, you've been drinking up all my mush-room ketchup !"

At a village church a clergyman friend of Sir George's had an organ constructed similarly to a musical-box, which the clerk had been taught to manipulate. Falling ill one Sunday, a member of the choir undertook to manage it. There were two sets of barrels, one with hymn tunes, the other with secular melodies. The clergyman, having given out the hymn, the organ at once struck up with " Drops o' Brandy," which, in spite of many attempts to stop it, it played to the end, and after a second's pause started off with another equally secular tune; until, in despair, the horrified churchwardens made their way to the vicar, and expostulated with the unhappy choir-man, who was helpless to remedy the unfortunate mistake he had made. Meanwhile the congregation was convulsed with laughter, more especially the younger portion of it. At last, in desperation, the officials procured four strong men, who carried the instrument bodily out of the church, so that it might finish its profanity among the tombs.

It was the custom of the Deans of Windsor, prior to Dean Wellesley, to invite the lay-clerks, once or twice a year, to dinner.

On one of these occasions the Dean said to Mr. Salmon, "What do you think of my celery?" or, as he pronounced it, "salary."

"Very good *indeed*, Mr. Dean."

"Ah!" said the Dean, "I raise it myself."

"Well, I wish you'd raise *mine*, Mr. Dean," retorted Salmon.

CHAPTER XXXIV.

DURING these happy years, until the death of Mrs. Savory in January, 1887, much of Sir George's time was spent, with Lady Elvey, at Buckhurst Park, interspersed with visits to the Isle of Wight and to Brocklesby.

While on one of these visits to the sea, Sir George wrote thus to a friend :

"The church we attend here is badly off for music, and the organist, who seems to have plenty of command of the instrument, cannot play a chant or hymn tune properly. He cannot keep quiet, but is always trying to embellish the music with runs and shakes ; he could not let even poor old Nare's ' Kyrie ' alone yesterday morning.

"The good old style of organ-playing is gone, thanks to C. C. instruments. I shall never be a convert to modern organs. They are a fearful mistake as regards Church music.

" I mourn over what's happened to my dear old friend at St. George's."

*   *   *   *   *

In 1885, Sir George and Lady Elvey had a very pleasant little visit to Mr. Slocock, when Sir George went to Newbury to conduct a concert for his friend and former pupil, Mr. Liddle, on the occasion of the bi-centenary of the birth of Handel and Bach. He was received with immense enthusiasm by the largest audience which has ever been gathered together at a concert there. The programme included Handel's " Ode on St. Cecilia's Day," with a miscellaneous second part. Miss Annie Marriott was the soprano, and Mr. T. Harpur the solo trumpet. Everything went exceedingly well.

Sir George at the rehearsal stopped to make the drummer tune more accurately, his naturally sensitive ear for pitch being unable to put up with a mere approximation.

From Newbury they drove to Wallingford, and were most kindly entertained by the clergyman and his wife. Here, also, Sir George conducted a concert for Mr. Liddle, when the " Messiah " was performed. On this occasion Harpur was engaged as before to play the trumpet, but, for the first time, this splendid performer failed. His death took place not long afterwards.

This year, also, was that of the Handel Festival, always of great interest to Sir George. He intensely enjoyed playing the violin; and Lady Elvey sung, with other members of the Bach Choir, in the chorus. About this time Sir George wrote the following interesting article, called forth by some remarks in the " Musical Standard."

" Handelian so-called Plagiarisms, Quotations and Adoptions.

" To the Editor of the ' Musical Standard.'

" Sir,

"As so much has been said and written about the so-called plagiarisms of Handel, I think the following quotation from Sir Joshua Reynolds's ' Lectures on Painting ' might be useful.

" ' When Raffaelle borrowed from Masaccio, he improved upon his model; but when he copied from the antique (as for the " Sacrifice at Lystra "), he took the whole much as it stands in the original. His known wealth was so great that he might borrow where he pleased without loss of credit.

The work from which he borrowed was public ; so that if he considered it a disgraceful theft, he was sure to be detected. But he was well satisfied that his character for invention would be little affected by such a discovery, nor is it, except in the opinion of those who are ignorant of the manner in which great works are built.'

" That Handel took subjects and ideas from other composers is an undeniable fact, but most of them he greatly improved. In some instances he took passages entire and unaltered, and in one case a whole movement, the chorus, ' Egypt was glad when they departed,' and, according to Dr. Crotch, these things should be considered as quotations from a well-known author, and not as plagiarisms which result from poverty of imagination and with the hope of escaping detection.

" I think we ought to feel grateful to Handel for using the fine fugue by Kerl for the chorus alluded to ; had he not done so, few would have ever known it.

" I cannot think it possible that anyone can entertain the opinion that the mighty giant was so destitute of inventive power that he was obliged to copy the works of other composers. I may add, it seems to be regarded by some as a crime, or sign of weakness, his having repeated his own subjects ; no one but the giant could have produced two such choruses as the ' Hallelujah' and the ' Horse and his rider' upon the same theme.

"Are there no imitators in the present day ? No copyists of Mendelssohn, Wagner, etc. ?

"I am, yours,

"HANDELIAN."

In connection with this, the following sentence occurs in a letter to a friend :

"Old Handel will not want a champion as long as I am alive."

May the day never come when Handel lacks a champion !

An honour it is to be of the number of these, when among them are Haydn, Mozart, Beethoven, Mendelssohn.

Haydn said, speaking of Handel, "He is the father of us all."

Mozart said, "Handel knows, better than any one of us, what is capable of producing a great effect. When he chooses he can strike like a thunderbolt."

Beethoven said, "He is the monarch of the musical kingdom.   He was the greatest composer that ever lived. I would uncover my head and kneel before his tomb."

Mendelssohn said, " Handel's works are treasures of sublimity and elevation."

Surely those who affect to despise Handel will not long wish to exclude themselves from the company of such an illustrious throng.

The following extracts from letters, which bear date about this period, will show that Sir George was not idle.

" *March 4th*, 1886.

" DEAR ———,

" I have been asked to arrange my anthem, ' Praise the Lord,' for instruments, for a choir festival at Brecon, and among the list of instruments I am to write for is the euphonium. I have not the least idea what sort of an instrument it is, but it is, I believe, used in military bands. What I want to know is, whether it plays tenor or bass parts, and also, whether I must write for it in the proper key, or whether transposition is necessary, and, if so, what key I ought to put the instrument into ?

" I do not intend to transpose the whole of my anthem for the convenience of Mr. Euphonium ;

so, if he cannot play like a good Christian in D, I shall dispense with his services.

*   *   *   *   *

" My compositions are a great trouble to me! and I am bothered with all sorts of questions, which I am expected to answer."

CHAPTER XXXV.

IN the spring of 1886, Sir George Martin Holloway begged Sir George to undertake the music for the opening of Holloway College. The proposal gave him great pleasure, as, in spite of the tremendous amount of work it entailed, he was delighted to prepare music once more to be performed in the presence of his beloved Queen. He not only undertook all the arrangements connected with the music, but composed and scored an " Ode " specially for the occasion.

On the opening day, after the service in the Chapel, when Her Majesty was in the Quadrangle, she was heard to ask, " Where is Sir George ? " and remarked, when he was pointed out to her conducting the band, " Oh ! yes, I see him ; there he is, as active as ever."

London, Reading, and Windsor, all furnished contingents for the chorus on this occasion, and whilst busily looking about for the various parties to give them instructions, Sir George came upon the Windsor group, to whom he said, "And where do you gentlemen come from?" "From Windsor, Sir George." "Ah!" said he, "*dear old Windsor,*—I need say nothing to *you.*"

Perhaps few, except those who have gone through it, are aware of the enormous amount of trouble it entails to get a satisfactory performance in a country place. Hours, and indeed weeks, were fully occupied in preparing and copying the music for the band. However, all seemed thoroughly satisfied with the result; but many sleepless nights testified to the strain felt by the veteran conductor. After the performance was over, having been without food from 9 a.m. to nearly the same hour at night—through some flaw in the arrangements, which in every other respect were so admirable—he was seized with a most alarming attack of illness, and great fears were entertained for his life. However, with prompt remedies, he soon rallied.

In the autumn of this year Sir George rented the vicarage of Melton Ross, in North Lincoln-shire, about a three miles' drive along the wolds from his brother-in-law's parish. The vicar thought it would be a great pleasure to his people if Sir George would sometimes preside at the organ, and asked him as a favour to do so. To this Sir George agreed, and, upon his arrival, sent to the schoolmistress, who acted as organist, to inquire what music was usually played. This lady could not bear the idea of being deposed, and would not consent to give up the organ unless she received special instructions direct from the vicar; so she stuck to her post, and not only played herself, but invited a friend to assist her, to the intense annoyance and disappointment of the principal members of the congregation. Mr. and Mrs. Webb, of Melton Ross, who could not show kindness enough to Sir George and Lady Elvey, came up and apologized, with not a little disgust, at the unseemly conduct of the organist, who, needless to relate, after she had been duly reprimanded for her conduct, gracefully retired from the organ-stool. While in Lincolnshire, Sir George always played for the evening service at Kirmington, and the simple country-folk would gather in the churchyard after service, and listen in wonder at the strains he drew from their little instrument.

He alludes to this in the following letter to his old pupil, Mr. Hancock:

> " Melton Ross Vicarage,
> > " Barnetby,
> > > "*Aug.* 31, 1886.

" MY DEAR HANCOCK,

" I have often longed to write to you for old acquaintance sake, but did not know your new address. Bransom told me what it was once, but I managed to forget it. We let our house, and have been at the above address since July 1st, but, according to our present plans, we shall return home on September 8th. I hope you are prospering at Leicester. It was reported some time ago that you were ill, but afterwards, I am glad to say, this report was proved to be false. I do not know that I have any news to communicate that will interest you at all. I have little to do with music now, but I play upon a small organ—six stops—when at home, and conduct the services at our iron church, about half a mile from our house, and during the time I have been here have played upon a small organ in Kirmington Church, which, you will remember, was built by your Leicester man (I forget his name). A nice little organ it is, but now the church is shut up for repairs, and the services are held in the school-room, where I play upon an organ with *one stop.*

" So you see what your old friend has come to !
I send you a copy of my ode,[1] very broad and
simple, but it answered the purpose for which
I composed it. I had rare hard work for the
occasion, and it was almost too much for me. Do
you remember my cantata for the Queen's Birthday? It was done at Windsor for their last
concert, and I conducted it. We had a fair string
band, and *some* wind instruments. I suppose
this will be my last appearance in the musical
world. I suppose next year will be a very loyal
one to all who live to see it. I shall at all times
be pleased to hear from you. . . .

" Ever yours sincerely,

" G. J. ELVEY."

*   *   *   *   *

The year 1887, which was anticipated with such
pleasure as that which would see the celebration of
Her Majesty's Jubilee, opened very sadly. Lady
Elvey's mother fell asleep in Jesus, early in
January.

She truly walked with God, and was a worthy
daughter of one of whom the poet Wordsworth
said, " She was a queen among women, one in
whose presence it was a privilege to sit."

[1] For the opening of Holloway College.

This was an intense grief to her daughter and to Sir George, as they were both devotedly attached to her. He alludes thus to it in a letter written at the time : " Lady Elvey lost her mother a short time since, and it is a very sad trial to both of us." Her loss seemed for a long time to cast a blank over their lives, as almost all their arrangements had been made with reference to her.

At Easter Sir George took great interest in arranging a performance of " The Messiah " in Ascot church. The chorus was composed of friends in the neighbourhood and some members of the Windsor and Eton Choral Society. At supper, after the performance, Sir George remarked the absence of one of the members, and inquiring as to its cause, was told that the absentee was suffering from gout. " What ! " he exclaimed in a tone of astonishment, almost of incredulity, " a member of the Windsor and Eton Choral Society got the *gout*." Then, as though nothing could be more satisfactory, " Things are looking up."

In May he visited Buxton to conduct his cantata,[1] which was to be performed at a concert got up by

[1] The one composed for Her Majesty's birthday in 1850.

his old pupil, Mr. Fred. Burgiss, organist of St. James's Church there.

From thence he and Lady Elvey went to Kendal, to stay with an uncle and aunt of the latter. The lovely scenery in the neighbourhood was a source of intense enjoyment to Sir George. This he saw to advantage, for the keen weather had covered the hills around Windermere with snow, and the reflection of a deep blue sky on their glistening surface enchanted him with its beauty.

While at Kendal Sir George was induced to give a short organ recital, to the immense pleasure of a large congregation assembled in the fine old parish church. This is claimed to be the largest in England, having five aisles.

Recitals in churches were a thing he would rarely give, as he held very strongly that organs were put there to assist men to worship God, and not for the glorification of the organist. After his death, Mr. Armstrong, the organist of Kendal, referring to this visit, wrote as follows to Lady Elvey.

"The loss of Sir George is deeply felt everywhere. We in Kendal always looked forward to his visits with real pleasure, and delighted to hear him on our parish church organ. Whenever I had the opportunity of attending the service at Windsor, during some twenty years or more, I was always impressed with the feeling that I was privileged to hear one of England's greatest church composers and cathedral organists, besides learning that Sir George was a good man, full of sympathy and kindness. It was a great happiness to me to meet with Sir George and yourself. I need not say that I shall always cherish a vivid recollection of him; indeed, who can forget him? He had many admirers too far away to know him personally.

"Yours very respectfully,

"W. B. ARMSTRONG."

On his return to Ascot Sir George prepared an anthem for his much-loved sovereign's jubilee. He also wrote two beautiful tunes to hymns by the Bishop of Exeter for the same occasion.

A copy of these he sent to the Queen, who graciously accepted them.

In June he went to Newbury to conduct the Jubilee celebration in the parish church there, where his Service in E and Jubilee anthem, " Behold, O God our Defender!" were to be performed. He played the organ at the previous

Sunday evening service, giving a short recital afterwards.

At the Jubilee service his conducting was full of energy and "go," and members of the orchestra and combined choirs who took part in the service still speak of its inspiriting nature.

Nothing annoyed him more than inanimate singing, and sensitive as his ear was, he has been heard to express preference for a certain singer, who he knew was frequently out of tune, over another who was mechanically perfect, but stiff and expressionless.

Greatly to his consternation, the Vicar of New-bury would not allow the usual drummer to play in church as he was a Dissenter, but Sir George, ever ready in an emergency, exclaimed to Lady Elvey, "We cannot do without the drums, so *you* must play them." Not a little to the amusement of many who attended the services, her ladyship wielded the drumsticks.

Sir George and Lady Elvey were, during this visit, most hospitably entertained by the Vicar of Newbury and his wife.

Two days afterwards Sir George was present in Windsor when Her Majesty returned from London and unveiled the statue on the Castle Hill. He was in the Quadrangle in the evening, when the Eton boys had their torchlight procession, and greatly enjoyed the picturesque sight.

He used to allude with pleasure to the fact of his having seen both the Queen's coronation and her jubilee.

Later in the summer Sir George had a very severe illness, and when partially recovered went with Lady Elvey to Lowestoft for a few weeks, and thence to the Isle of Wight. Here he greatly enjoyed the company of two of his nieces, and used to have tremendous fun over his daily *régime* of milk pudding, which he nicknamed "Slobbery Boski." He would often send for the landlady, and amid much laughter inform her that he was tired of "slobbery boski," and must have some apple tart or plum pudding.

With children he was always the same, and many of his little nephews and nieces received from him amusing nicknames. One little girl he would persist in calling "Dick," and though frequently remonstrated with on the subject, he refused laughingly to alter his opinion, saying that as she had short hair he never *could* remember that she was not a boy. He would often keep these little people very merry by inquiring if they knew how to make a cherub, and when they replied in the negative, he promptly showed them—of course all immediately going through the same performance. He would then show them how a jackdaw looked down a bone, and many other tricks, at which there would be peals of laughter.

He had a really curious way of putting into words the thoughts which he assumed to be occupying the minds of people on certain occasions. One afternoon the following remarks afforded the hearer much amusement, chiefly from the manner in which the last sentence was spoken: "Oh! how d'ye do?" etc., etc. "Lady Elvey is not at home this afternoon. She's at Windsor—gone *shopping*. I'd rather not go when there's much shopping to be done—particularly in Windsor. You see I lived there a good many years, and it's not very pleasant to loiter about. People look at one as much as to say, 'Ugh! *You* come back again!'"

CHAPTER XXXVI.

IN June, 1888, he took part for the last time in the Handel Festival, playing his violin at the same desk with Dr. Longhurst of Canterbury.

In view of this, he had been looking through a copy of the autograph score of the " Messiah," with the result given in his own words below :

" To the Editor of the ' Musical Times.'

" SIR,

" It always seemed to me a singular thing that in the arrangement of the 'Pastoral' Symphony Handel should have doubled the second violin part only. A short time since, in looking at the autograph score published by the Sacred Harmonic Society, I discovered that he had written a third violin part to play in octaves to the first violin, so that both first and second violin parts were doubled. Upon making this discovery I wrote to Sir Frederick Ouseley, and he told me that he pos-

THE TOWERS, WINDLESHAM.

From a photograph by Hills and Saunders.

sessed the score from which Handel conducted the 'Messiah,' and this has the third violin part to the Symphony, and further, that this part is also in the copy at the Foundling Hospital.

"On learning these facts I wrote to Mr. Manns, and am happy to say that at the recent Handel Festival the Symphony was performed in the way the giant intended it to be, and I hope it will never be again performed otherwise.

"I am, yours truly,

"G. J. ELVEY.

"*July* 18*th*, 1888."

Throughout this year much time was occupied in searching the neighbourhood for a suitable house, as the lease of "La Tour" had nearly expired. In the autumn a pretty place within easy reach of Windsor was secured, and the removal took place in June of the ensuing year.

During the last years of his life Sir George much appreciated the beautiful surroundings and the repose of his country home, and these years were probably among the happiest he ever spent.

Long drives through the lovely Swinley woods, or across Chobham Common, were the greatest delight to him, especially in the long summer evenings, when Nature, in the fading light, looked her best.   Many pleasant hours were spent in this way, and, with a true artist's eye, Sir George took a keen delight in pointing out to visitors picturesque "bits," and the best points from which to see any particularly lovely view.

In the summer of 1890 his only daughter, Nellie, was married to Leonard Creasy, and in November she left with her husband for his home in Ceylon. Sir George greatly felt the parting, as he knew it would be a final one.

In July he and Lady Elvey started on a driving tour from their home to Cromer, stopping at various places *en route*.   After a glorious day, just before reaching Hitchin, they were overtaken by a tremendous storm, and before shelter was reached were all tolerably well drenched.   The rain came down in torrents for about six hours, till the water ran in the streets like rivers.   However, happily for the tourists, the next day was fine, and the journey was continued to Cambridge, where Sir George thoroughly enjoyed seeing the colleges, and, as they remained over Sunday, he was enabled to attend the services in King's and Trinity College Chapels.

Another week or so spent in this way, driving

by easy stages through part of Cambridgeshire and Norfolk, brought them to Cromer.

Their visit here was a very pleasant one. Mr. and Mrs. Johnson were staying next door, and Sir George used to enjoy a pipe with his friend and a stroll on the cliff when he felt the steep descent to the beach beyond his power. The afternoons were spent in long drives through the Norfolk lanes.

On one occasion, during this visit, a " gentle-man " called to request him to patronize a concert to be given in the Town Hall, arranged by himself and his brothers. He consented, and great was his amusement when he found that the "gentle-man" was one of three niggers who gave daily entertainments on the shore !

Towards the close of September, fearing that the cold equinoctial gales, which are experienced with peculiar force at that, the most exposed part of the east coast, would be dangerous for Sir George's health, at the kind invitation of Mrs. Bush they went to East Cowes Park for a fortnight, spending there a very happy time. Sir George passed many pleasant hours boating and fishing in the Solent, and in taking long drives in the island. He was deeply interested in Mrs. Bush's aged uncle, Dr. Moore, who for many years had been tutor to the Maharajah of Johore in India, but was now a bedridden invalid. Whenever the old man was equal to seeing visitors, Sir George would seat himself at his bedside, and earnestly strive to win him to full and simple trust in the Saviour.

At the harvest festival at Trinity Church, West Cowes, Sir George played the service, and gave a recital afterwards, which was a source of much pleasure to the congregation.

The organ he described as "a box of tricks;" for it had been built with all kinds of contrivances to suit a lame organist.

The following summer a visit was made to Kendal, which was endeared to Lady Elvey by many pleasant associations. It was there that her mother had been brought up, and many members of the family still resided in the district.

After a few weeks spent in Lake-land, they went on to Penmaenmawr, stopping at Lancaster, Chester, and Colwyn Bay *en route*.

For two or three winters previous to his death, Sir George had been forbidden by his doctor to spend as much time as formerly out of doors. He greatly missed his usual occupation of superintending all that was done in his garden, but, with the gentleness and power of adapting himself to circumstances that was so strongly characteristic of him, he gave up what had hitherto been such a delight, and spent his time chiefly in his little study, reading for hours together, and writing letters.

He took an intense interest in all the topics of the day, was always well up in all parliamentary news, and carefully studied the musical papers.

During these quiet years of his retirement he devoted a great deal of time to looking over his music, and preparing some for publication.

A short time after he left Windsor he published his popular anthem for Palm Sunday, " In the Third Hour." When first he wrote this, the Dean and Chapter of Windsor were much exercised in their minds as to whether it was quite suitable for performance in church, the subject being treated rather dramatically.   However, it was decided upon, and Bishop Thirlwall of St. David's, who was present on its first introduction, wrote thus of it to a friend :

" Abergwili Palace,
" 17th April, 1867.

".   .   .   .

" After breakfast the Queen sent me a message by the Dean of Windsor that she was very sorry she should not be able to attend the twelve o'clock service, and asking me to send her the MS. of my sermon, which of course I did as soon as it was discharged.

" The afternoon was very pleasantly divided between the library, magnificent Oriental MSS., and rare miniatures, and St. George's Chapel, and a wonderful dramatic anthem, which, though arranged by Dr. Elvey, I believe to be of mediæval origin, being a musical picture of the Crucifixion."

" How the Bishop came to attribute a mediæval origin to the anthem," said Sir George recently to a friend, " I cannot say. No piece of that description ever came under my observation."

Not long after his youngest son Handel's birth, he wrote a fugue on the initials of his name, G. F. H. E., which he has left carefully for him to have when he is old enough.

Among other musical work at this time he prepared his violin and piano gavotte for publication.

In the letter which accompanied a copy sent to a friend, the following sentence occurs : " I send you a chip from the very old block, which I have been foolish enough to publish."

He also prepared one of his services and wrote
a Communion Service. Besides all these, he composed a great number of hymn tunes for various
collections.

The last of them was written not many months
before his death for a Scotch hymn-book. One
was a funeral hymn, and this he arranged somewhat elaborately, and spent much time and trouble
over it.

He always said, when engaged on the work,
that he felt he was composing his requiem.

The long list of compositions at the end of this
volume will show what a voluminous and versatile
composer was Sir George. What is more remarkable still, is that he excelled in any branch of
the art to which he directed his attention. His
musical ideas flowed with marvellous rapidity, and
it appeared to take but a few moments, when
suitable words presented themselves to his mind,
before they were reproduced in a musical picture.
Sometimes this would happen while taking a drive,
a country walk, or when sitting quietly over a
cigar. Then he would take a piece of music-
paper, and, in a few minutes (for he wrote with
wonderful celerity), his thoughts would take
legible form.

He never left home without carefully packing some music-paper, for composition was to him a form of recreation.

The following letters written to a friend, one referring to an article in the " Musical World," are interesting as giving his opinion on modern organs and modern organ-playing.

" DEAR ————,

" Although I am now living a very quiet life, and have no musical occupation, I like to know what is going on in the musical world, and read with much interest the account of organ recitals from the paper which some kind friend sends me.

" Now I very much regret to find so few of Handel's choruses played. Can you account for it ? Probably I stand alone, but I prefer the old G or F organs (as St. George's used to be); they are, in my opinion, more suitable for Church music.[1]

[1] Sir George, while preferring the G or F organ for his own use, as he had always been accustomed to it, did not so much object to C organs when on a large scale, and frequently played on them in various parts of the country. But he certainly did object to this compass in small organs, in which, often, there is no stop on the pedals but the one Bourdon, and the organist is thus deprived of the power to efficiently support the voices. During

Gibbons in F, that service of services, on my old instrument, where every stop went down to F, will not be forgotten by me, and possibly by others.

"What an absurdity it is to find in a village church a C C organ, with pedals up to your neck, for hymns and chants! Verily the world has gone mad, and organ-playing too—Pedals! pedals!! pedals!!!—nothing but pedals.

" I sometimes wish organs were made without them; we should then have appropriate music played in our churches.

" I was very much amused with an article in the 'Musical World' a short time since, 'The way we write our oratorios.' I wish the author of it would say something about modern organ performances. He might be able to tell us how many notes could be played in a second."

"Sir,

" I would crave the indulgence of a small space in your columns, not only to express my own

the latter part of his life Sir George inclined to have equal temperament, but his nervousness prevented him from having this alteration made; for, if he had not after all been satisfied with the result, the older form could not have been returned to.

opinions, but to gain, if possible, the views of those amongst your readers who may think the great subject a worthy one for your consideration. This I do, not with a desire for controversy on my part, as that I entirely leave to others, but I would much wish to ask—What are organs put into churches for? and for what use were they originally intended? It seems to me that only one answer can be given to these questions; for surely the purpose was and ought to be for playing the Church services. But, Sir, can anyone affirm that in the present day this is the all-important use of the instrument? Dr. Beattie in his 'Essays' says, 'the sound of an organ puts us in mind of a church, and that sound should serve before all things to bring to the human heart and mind the words, the prayers, the praises, and the comfort which it aids us to express in the true and reasonable services of the Church.' It appears to me, however, that in these days organ recital is the chief use of the church organ, and I would here protest against the modern C C compass of this once noble instrument. I am fully aware that Bach's pedal fugues cannot be played on G organs, but there are many grand compositions which can be better performed on G than on C C organs, and Handel's six organ fugues were written for the G organ. Depend upon it, Sir, our forefathers were not such fools as many suppose them to have been, and they had good and wise reasons for extending the manuals to G, and in some instances to F F.

" In expressing these opinions I know that I may meet with severe treatment, but although I may stand alone now, it was not always so. Many dear friends who have passed away entertained the same opinions as myself, and I, alone or not, cannot but utter a cry of lament for the past grandeur and the present weakness of our dear and valued instrument."

" When once Church music became the subject of conversation," writes a friend, " Sir George entered into it with keenness and animation. The hearer, if he knew little or nothing of music and its history, might feel that he was incapable of duly appreciating so great a treat, and that he was now being justly punished for having neglected this branch of his education. But that there was anything dull or prosy about the conversation he could not feel. Even if it developed for a short time into a monologue, the earnest, unaffected manner of the speaker combined with the absence of technical terms put him at his ease and made him at least *think* he understood, while the enthusiasm and the deeply devotional spirit which breathed in every word, aroused within him a feeling of admiration and respect."

Sir George was fond of quoting a remark of his brother's, relating to style in Church music. He considered that our fine old cathedrals and their music ought to go together—the music should suggest worship just as much as roof and arch and window. A stranger listening at a distance and unable to catch the words, should be able to say, " That is sacred music." The foregoing will show that though in a sense his public life was over, he had lost none of his keen interest in the world in which he had played such a prominent part.

But the stress of public work and the toil of a busy life was over, and for him had come a well-earned period of repose—a life so peaceful that it seemed as if nothing could mar its deep content and calm.

This is beautifully described by Mr. Curwen in an article which appeared in " The Musical Herald," and in the letter which follows :

" The flicker of the fire catches one's gaze, and stirs the imagination ; we seem to see the long procession of Anglican Church composers, loyal, earnest and devout, in the pursuit of sacred art.

" The impression we retain is of an old man sitting opposite to us, who knows and embodies more completely than anyone living the traditions of the Anglican school—a man who has lived a life as earnest and devout and true as those of any of the musicians who have preceded him."

" It was a pleasure to me, living as I do in the stress of modern musical life, its competitions and jealousies, the pushing and striving of rival men and rival schools of composition, to meet with one who breathed a calmer air. Sir George was like a warrior who had laid down his arms; he had no jealousies, and was full of charitable judgments, while his musical faith was surely fixed in the grand old models in which he had been reared— Handel's and the best of the Anglican Church school of composers. Now and then, as we talked, some topic would rouse him, and he would deliver a vigorous opinion, but immediately he would add, ' Don't put that down,' so afraid was he of hurting anyone's feelings, so reluctant to enter the arena of controversy with which he had done."

CHAPTER XXXVII.

IN 1892 Ilfracombe was chosen for the annual summer outing, and many excursions were made to the different points of interest along the rugged, wave-worn coast.

During these later years two visits were made to Bristol, on both occasions for the purpose of attending concerts at which some of Sir George's music was to be performed, and gratifying indeed was the reception he met with in that city.

The first time was to attend a concert given by the Orpheus Glee Society, at which his part-song for men's voices, " From yonder rustling mountain," was most exquisitely performed. So delighted was he with this concert, that when the same society gave a performance at St. James's Hall, he went again to hear them there. The last time he and Lady Elvey visited the city was to attend a concert of the Madrigal Society, in which he had always taken a great interest.

For many years he went regularly to Bristol for

their " Ladies' Nights," taking with him his two head boys. On these occasions he, Dr. Corfe, and Mr. Rootham, used to sing side by side amongst the basses.

At the concert in April, 1892, the society sung his fine part-song, " The Zetland Fishermen." Of this performance it was said: " The bright and sparkling song of the ' Zetland Fishermen,' by the veteran Sir George Elvey, who occupied a seat in the balcony, is full of clever and effective writing. The treatment of the phrases, ' We'll sing while we bait ' and ' We'll sing while we haul,' is nautical in every sense of the word. The piece had evidently received very careful attention at the rehearsals; hence its many beauties were adequately portrayed. So delighted were the assemblage with the composition and its rendering, that it was followed by a hearty burst of applause, which was continued until the composer had acknowledged the compliment, and the pitch-pipe was blown for a repetition of the charming work."

Sir George was delighted with the performance, and said to Mr. Rootham, " I do not expect to hear it again, but the last time is the best."

Mr. Rootham says : " I never remember the whole of the members of the society being more pleased than they were on this occasion. To feel that we all had been the means of giving our dear old friend a musical treat, was a source of unfeigned gratification to every member of the society, boys as well as men, and I shall never forget the kind way in which he spoke of the whole performance."

After the concert Sir George and Lady Elvey were most hospitably entertained by Mr. and Mrs. Harvey, and one present during the evening says of Sir George, " His large fund of anecdotes upon musical matters, and his kind, genial manner, made that evening one that will ever bring back a pleasant recollection with it."

Sir George had anticipated with great pleasure meeting at Bristol his kind old friend, Mr. Blair-Oliphant, and it was a great disappointment to him to hear from his brother-in-law there, that he was seriously ill. The arrangement to meet at Bristol had been of long standing, as the concert had been originally fixed for January, but was postponed on account of the death of the Duke of Clarence.

The last performance in which he took part was in April, 1893, when for the last time he conducted the work he always loved, Handel's " Messiah."

For this he conducted all the practices, and stood during the whole of the concert, which was a great success; in fact, it was considered unequalled in that part of the world.

Referring to this, he wrote thus to Mr. Hancock :

"The Towers,
"Windlesham.

"MY DEAR HANCOCK,

"I am much pleased to find from the paper that you have sent me, your services have been so highly appreciated, and I congratulate you most heartily. I am in the thick of getting up the "Messiah." The performance is to come off on the 29th. In a place like this, where we are so far from everyone, it is a difficult matter. We have an amateur band and chorus. . . .

"I am,

"Your old friend,

"G. J. ELVEY."

In June a last pleasant visit was made to Brocklesby, and later on Sir George and Lady Elvey, with the "little chap," again visited Penmaenmawr.

He seemed stronger than on the previous occasion, and spent many long days driving to see various points of interest in the neighbourhood. In this way Beaumaris, Bangor, Lake Ogwen, Trefrew, Llanrwst, and many other places were visited.

Every morning, as Lady Elvey and Handel returned from their early bathe, Sir George would be out watching for them at the top of the hill.

The church services here were a great pleasure to him, and at the harvest festival one of his anthems was performed, in which he took great interest, attending a rehearsal.

On his return from Wales everyone was struck by his healthful appearance, and indeed he seemed better able to take exercise, and in every way stronger than for many previous years.

Walking was always a pleasure to him, and early in life he was a great pedestrian, yet he never cared to go out alone, being intensely nervous of strange dogs. He often graphically described the terror he once suffered at the Castle, when, left waiting in a large room, he spied, as the door closed, a collie—the only occupant of the apartment—looking at him with anything but friendly eyes.

This fear seems somewhat curious, as he was very fond of animals, and generally had a pet dog of his own.

At this time he greatly interested himself in endeavours to reclaim some property for a poor woman, which she had unfortunately lost. He was ever ready to perform a kindness for a fellow creature, and this effort cost many hours of letter-writing, which, owing to his failing eyesight, was to him a fatiguing task. He also took a journey to Windsor simply to further this object.

Soon after he received a terrible shock, to which he several times alluded, saying he had never got over it. The " little chap " was having a romp in the passage, and in trying to save himself from falling, dashed his hand through a glass door leading into the hall. The crash was tremendous, but the child did not utter a sound until he saw the blood streaming down, and then he said to his mother, "I am killed, I am killed!" Still his first thought was that his father should not be alarmed ; but, unfortunately, Sir George came in search of Lady Elvey, while she was trying to stop the bleeding and bandage the dreadful wounds.

The shock brought on such a fit of trembling that it was some time before Sir George recovered. In connection with this, it may be mentioned, in illustration of his excessive nervousness and sensitiveness, that he could never read the account of an accident in the paper, or pass a butcher's shop without shuddering.

This extreme sensitiveness had been strongly characteristic of him all his life, for one of his earliest pupils writes as follows :

"One afternoon I was in the organ-loft, and I noticed he was *indeed* very nervous. When I asked him the reason, he told me the anthem was 'Worthy is the Lamb,' and the 'Amen' chorus from the 'Messiah,' and, he added, 'I can never play this without trembling. If you see me going to break down, hit me hard between the shoulders.' But though I could see how the music affected him, all went well."

CHAPTER XXXVIII.

TOWARDS the end of October he made a great effort to be present at a concert given by the St. George's Choir at the Albert Institute, when his prize part-song, " O power supreme," was given. This was exceedingly well sung, and gave him great pleasure. A well-known newspaper thus wrote after his death : " Only six weeks ago he conducted a glee of his own composition at the Windsor St. George's Choir concert, and looked lovely, with his snow-white locks and sturdy, vigorous figure, like a grand old polar bear, on the platform, where he was greeted with roars of applause."

During the last two winter seasons an orchestral class was held in his drawing-room every Monday, conducted by Mr. Arthur Blagrove. In this he took considerable interest, and only the Monday before his death came in to play the piano, while his " Christmas Bells " was being rehearsed, in preparation for a concert which was to have been held on Tuesday, December 19th.

For long years his deep religious feelings formed such an integral part of his character that no one could be long in his presence without being impressed by the absolute reality of his religion, and his humble, simple trust in his Saviour.

As the peaceful evening of his life drew to its close, his gentle spirit seemed to dwell more and more on things above.

A gentleman who had not long known him, and was perhaps one that would scarcely have been expected to notice it, was so impressed by this, that, speaking of him after his death, he said, " No one could be long in his presence without being struck by his devout, religious spirit."

Many speak of the influence of his music on the world, but though this was great, how much greater still was the influence of his gentle temper and holy life upon all with whom he came in contact !

His compositions can certainly lose nothing in the estimation of those who were privileged to hear his conversation.

His quiet unobtrusive piety showed itself continually in little things, and possibly its sincerity was thus made the more remarkable. A guest at his table has been impressed by the reverent manner in which he said grace ; and so it was at all times, in a thousand indefinable ways, he unconsciously became a teacher of religion and morality.

How well in his case might the lines of Longfellow be applied :

> " God sent his singers upon earth
> With songs of sadness and of mirth,
> That they might touch the hearts of men,
> And bring them back to heaven again."

It was beautiful and wonderful to see a man who, for the greater part of his long life, had given his heart to God, using all the best gifts with which he was endowed to promote His glory in public worship, and by his holy influence, and gentle words dropped in season, seeking to lead others to the Saviour.

Although so humble and retiring, he yet lost no opportunity of trying to win souls for Christ ; by the bedside of the dying, among the labourers or servants he employed, and in letters to old pupils and friends, he constantly urged the importance of being ready for eternity.

As an instance of these "words in season," the following letter, written by one of his old pupils after his death, and quoting a passage contained in one of Sir George's letters to him, may be interesting :

" The following words of Christian hope and resignation contained in one of his last letters to me may well serve as a fitting 'cadence' to a useful and well-spent life (written on the occasion of his 73rd birthday).

" ' I am an old man now, having entered my 73rd year. . . . A birthday at my time of life is a solemn affair; I trust when the end comes I may "depart in peace," and fall asleep in Jesus. Amen.' "

From another letter (to a private pupil) the following is taken :

" DEAR ——,

" I pray that your future may be full of happiness ; but, after all, this life is only a preparation for another more glorious one. May we all be partakers of the Heavenly inheritance !

" When Mr. —— read the lessons last Sunday, I could not help thinking of the grand and blessed future when he read, ' As we have borne the image of the earthy, we shall also bear the image of the Heavenly." . . .

The following touching letter was written to the daughter of one who had been his dearest friend:

"December 28th, 1891.

"My dear Mrs. ——,

"From the last report sent me by Miss ——, I felt the end of my dear and valued friend was near, so I was prepared for the receipt of the sad news you have sent me this morning. It is sad to me, for I have lost one with whom I have been acquainted for more than fifty years. We have, as you know, been like brothers; both of us have gone through many trials, and sympathized with each other. His loss is a great one to me; such a friend it does not fall to the lot of many to possess in this cold world. But we have cause to rejoice, too; we know full well the dear one is in peace and in perfect happiness; he having served and loved the Lord Jesus on earth, is now in the arms of the Saviour for ever and ever. It is a warning for me to be prepared to follow, and my end cannot be far off. I hope you will always think of me, and that you and Mr. —— will not forget me in your prayers. I shall be afraid to venture to be present on Wednesday; the service would be too much for me, and I am fearful of getting a chill. The weather is very trying, and I seldom go out.

" How touching the account you have given me of the end! That smile you will never forget. Your letter came when I was having my morning's reading; I instantly turned to 1 Thess. iv. 13.

" May God comfort and bless you all for Christ's sake. Amen.

> " I am,
>
> " Yours sincerely,
>
> (Signed) "G. J. ELVEY."

*   *   *   *   *

Little wonder that people speak of the " beauty of his playing, peculiarly his own," but in truth the fingers were but the channel of the rapture of his soul. A young girl once entered the Chapel, and was so impressed by this feeling as to remark, " The way the Psalms are played here is a commentary on the words."

An artist, meeting Lady Elvey shortly after Sir George's death, made use of the same expression when referring to his playing.

It was his usual habit to rise early, to gain half

an hour's quiet reading and prayer before family worship or the duties of the day commenced, and as he felt the end was nearing he devoted more and more time to the earnest study of his Bible, every verse of which was the subject of much careful thought.

During the last few weeks of his life intense was his delight in reading Ryle on St. John. In speaking of himself he often said, "I have no wonderful Christian experience to relate, but I trust that my sins are forgiven through the precious blood of Christ."

Living in the country, two miles from any place of worship, it was impossible in bad weather for anyone to go to church on Sunday, and on these occasions he would gather all the household together, and himself read the service, play the chants and hymns, and read some beautiful address, upon which he would not infrequently make earnest remarks of his own.

Such a service he held only ten days before his death.

Truly his was a beautiful old age! Happy and devout, he peacefully waited his call. On Tuesday afternoon, December 5th, he was not very well, but it did not appear to be more than a passing attack of indigestion such as he sometimes had. Although Lady Elvey proposed to stay at home with him, and not go to London, as she had planned, he overruled her misgivings, and persuaded her to carry out her intention. He appeared fairly well, and on her return for late dinner he took his meal with heartiness, and appeared quite himself again.

On Wednesday he was seized with a severe attack of illness, and Lady Elvey was greatly alarmed to find that he could not walk or do anything without assistance. At his own desire, however, he was dressed and helped downstairs to his favourite chair in the study.

He remained up till about three o'clock, and then retired to bed, from which he never again rose. He was so feeble that he could not turn, but always said he was comfortable and had no pain.

In the evening, in response to a telegram, his son Robert arrived, and he roused somewhat, and seemed pleased to see him. The following day he rallied a little, and had more strength ; but the fever returned at night, and in the morning, though that was conquered, it was apparent that it would be very difficult at his age to rally him from the excessive weakness that influenza had left.

About seven o'clock on Saturday morning, without pain or suffering of any kind, with one bright look, his spirit fled to be with the Saviour he had loved so long.

Throughout his illness his thoughts were all for others, lamenting that one or two who came to see him should have such a dull time. He feared that Lady Elvey would be knocked up, and frequently desired that she would go to bed, feeling grieved that he should give so much trouble.

As regards himself, his mind seemed in perfect peace, and we can but praise God for His mercy in sparing one of his highly-strung temperament all fear and suffering. Nothing could exceed the care and thought shown to him by the servants, who were, one and all, devoted to their master, and no words can express the unremitting care and attention of his medical attendant, who acted on many occasions both as nurse and doctor.

* * * * *

On Thursday, December 14th, he was laid to rest—"until the day break and the shadows flee away"—in the catacombs of St. George's, close under the walls of the noble Chapel which had been the scene of his life-work.

The whole ceremony was a very simple, but

a very impressive one. By order of Her Majesty the Queen the grave was lined with exquisite white camellias and chrysanthemums from the royal conservatories.

The remains were met at the north door of the Chapel by the Bishop of Rochester, the Dean of Windsor, and Bishop Barry, and as they were borne through the nave to the garter-bannered choir the opening sentences of the burial service were chanted to Croft's music by the choir, Sir Walter Parratt conducting.

Sir Joseph Savory followed as chief mourner, representing Lady Elvey, who was prevented from being present by an attack of influenza.

The Queen was represented by Colonel the Hon. W. Carington.

The Dean of Windsor and Bishop Barry took the service inside the Chapel, the latter reading the lesson.

The music consisted of the Thirty-ninth Psalm (Purcell), and Sir George's own touching anthem, " The souls of the righteous," which he had composed for the service held in the Private Chapel in memory of H.R.H. Princess Alice, on December 18th, 1878.

As the procession left the Chapel a funeral

march was played, and the hymn sung at the grave-side by the famous choir, "over which he presided so splendidly for so many years," was his own setting of " Just as I am, without one plea." This was the most touching part of the service, and the crowd standing round were visibly moved.

Among the immense congregation who filled the choir and nave were Dr. Lloyd, Dr. Verrinder, Dr. Bridge, Sir John Stainer, Dr. Hubert Parry, Sir Arthur Sullivan, Dr. Turpin, Dr. Arnold, etc.

Throughout it was a scene that touched the historic sense.

Many "old boys" and men now prominent in the musical world, who had been Sir George's pupils, were present.

What a rush of memories must have come upon them as they sat in the softened light of the winter afternoon, waiting for the service to begin !

Memories of happy days spent in the royal borough twenty, thirty, or perhaps forty years ago, under the guidance of one at whose grave they met that day—one to whose kindly nature they all owed much, and whom they would ever remember with a feeling of tender reverence and affection.

His loss had snapped a link with the past—

a past of all that was best and noblest in English Church music and English Church musicians, and the pathetic sadness of old association clung round the severed chain.

The " old boys "—some of them with grey hair —sent a wreath in memory of their "grand old master," and at the " White Hart," where the friends from a distance assembled after the ceremony, many and gentle were the reminiscences awakened.

A friend of Sir George's wrote the following testimony to his life-work after his death :

" Music is the most ennobling gift when used aright, and to the glory of God. Sir George's work was so much *that*, and the memory of services at Windsor years ago are some of my happiest recollections."

CHAPTER XXXIX.

THUS runs the simple story of a simple life. No one met Sir George Elvey at any time during his career but was struck with the intense passionate love of the man for his work, and for the holy zeal and conscientiousness that characterized the simplest details of his daily life. The soul of the man breathed through his music, and his music was such as made for righteousness. From a boy his life was marked by gentleness, purity, and unswerving consistency to the Master whom he loved, and lived to serve. And in his later years, when honours fell thick upon him, amid the glamour of the Court and the loud shout of public applause, his ears were never dulled to the whisperings of the still small voice.

It was his delight that his best and noblest efforts should have been devoted to the musical adaptation of divine themes. And now that he has 'gone from us, the memory of his life-work cannot die.

It is enshrined upon the altars of our national religion itself.

" The shadow is gone down upon the dial of thy days,
No more thy once familiar form moves in the busy crowd of
      men.
Thou art at rest ;
The tear thy memory demands
Is paid by those who loved thee best.
Good-bye awhile, dear, kind old man ;
In happier scenes than these we'll meet and love again."

APPENDIX.

LIST OF GEORGE J. ELVEY'S COMPOSITIONS.

ORGAN.

" Christmas Bells."   Impromptu.

" Festal March."

" A wet day at Henley " (unpublished).

Several voluntaries published in collections.

SERVICES.

Te Deum and Benedictus in F.

Magnificat and Nunc Dimittis in F.

Te Deum, Jubilate, and Kyrie in B flat.

Cantate Domino and Deus Misereatur in D.

The Office for the Holy Communion in E, including Benedictus and Agnus Dei.

Magnificat and Nunc Dimittis in E.

Benedictus and Agnus Dei in E.

Kyrie Eleison in B flat.

Evening Service in E, eight voices (unpublished).

Evening Service in C major (unpublished).

ANTHEMS.

"And it was the third hour."

"Arise, shine, for thy light is come."

"Arise, shine, for thy light is come," longer (unpublished).

· "Almighty and everlasting God" (composed for the opening of St. Michael's College, Tenbury).

"Blessed are they that fear the Lord."

"Bow down Thine ear" (Gresham Prize Medal).

"Behold, O God our Defender" (Jubilee Anthem).

"Blessed are the dead."

"Christ being raised from the dead."

"Come, Holy Ghost, our souls inspire."

"Come unto Me, all ye that labour."

"Daughters of Jerusalem."

"Hear, O heavens!" (unpublished).

"Hide not Thou Thy face" (unpublished).

"In that day shall this song be sung."

"I beheld, and lo! a great multitude."

"I was glad when they said."

"If we believe that Jesus died."

"I will alway give thanks" (unpublished).

"My God, my God!"

"O! do well unto Thy servant."

"O! give thanks unto the Lord."

"O! be joyful in God."

"O! be joyful in the Lord, all ye lands."

"O Holy Ghost, our souls inspire!"

"O praise the Lord of Heaven!"

"O ye that love the Lord!"

"O praise the Lord! all ye heathen" (for three choirs, unpublished).

"O Lord! from Whom."

"O worship the Lord!"

" Praise the Lord, ye servants " (unpublished).

" Praise the Lord, and call upon His name."

" Rejoice in the Lord " (for the re-opening of the organ, St. George's Chapel).

" Sing, O heavens ! " (unpublished).

" Sing unto God !" (unpublished).

" This is the day which the Lord hath made."

" The ways of Zion do mourn " (composed for his Mus. Doc. degree, unpublished).

" The eyes of all wait on Thee " (Harvest Anthem, unpublished).

" The Lord is King" (unpublished).

" They that go down to the sea " (unpublished).

" The Lord is my light and my salvation" (unpublished).

"Teach me, O Lord !" (unpublished).

" The souls of the righteous."

" Unto Thee have I cried."

" Wherewithal shall a young man."

" While shepherds watched " (unpublished).

" When Israel came out of Egypt" (unpublished).

" Come, ye lofty" (Christmas Carol).

"Come, ye nations, thankful own " (Christmas Hymn).

"Thou art gone to the grave" (Funeral Hymn).

"To thee, O Lord! we bring this day" (Baptismal Hymn).

Two Chorales { " I shall not in the grave remain." / " To Thee, O Lord! I yield my spirit."

CHANTS.

Fifteen Double Chants.
Thirty Cathedral Chants.

ORCHESTRAL.

"Mount Carmel," Oratorio (unpublished).
"The Resurrection and Ascension," Oratorio (unpublished).
Cantata for Her Majesty's Birthday.
"Hark! what tumultuous sounds" (Cantata for William IV.'s Birthday, 1836).
"Victoria" (Ode).
"The British Lion sleeps."
"The British Sacred Banner."
"The Festal March."
"The Albert Edward March."

"Rejoice in the Lord." ⎫
"Sing unto God."
"The ways of Zion."
"Behold, O God our Defender."
"In that Day."
"The Lord is King." ⎬ Anthems.
"Sing, O Heavens!"
"The Lord is my Light and my Salvation."
"Praise the Lord, and call upon His name."
"This is the day which the Lord hath made."
"O be joyful in the Lord." ⎭
"Let us now praise famous men."

PIANO.

"The Albert Edward March."

"Christmas Bells."

"Festal March."

"Gavotte à la mode ancienne."

PIANO AND VIOLIN.

Introduction and Gavotte.

PART SONGS.

"Britannia rules by land and sea."

"Bridal bells" (unpublished).

"British sacred banner" (unpublished).

"Bright may the sun shine o'er him" (unpublished).

"From yonder rustling mountain."

"Gather ye rosebuds" (unpublished).

"Love, under friendship's" (unpublished).

"Ode to the North-west wind."

"The thorn is in the bud" (unpublished).

"Softly, softly blow, ye breezes."

"The Zetland Fishermen" (unpublished).

"Shall I wasting in despair" (unpublished).

"Hark! those voices sweetly blending."

"Victoria," an Ode.

"O, Power supreme!"

SONGS.

"Who can see thee, dearest child?"

"Caliban" (unpublished).

CHISWICK PRESS:—CHARLES WHITTINGHAM AND CO.
TOOKS COURT, CHANCERY LANE, LONDON.

9 783337 095079